EASY

MONEY

& OTHER

STORIES

EASY MONEY

& OTHER STORIES

by Steve Potter

Dedicated, in memoriam, to the real Muscles.

Thanks to *the force that through the green fuse drives the flower* for everything. Thanks to Mom and Dad for getting the whole "me" thing started. Thanks to friends, family members, and coworkers without whom I may never have encountered the real-life inspirations for Tiny, Scooter, Babydoll, and others. Thanks to great teachers through the years in particular: Mrs. Steinberg and Mrs. Dankner at Oceanside Public Grammar School # 5; Dr. and Mrs. Lawson at SUNY, Oneonta; Joseph McElroy, Marie Ponsot, and William S. Wilson at Queens College, CUNY. Thanks to Phoebe Bosche, Matt Briggs, Stacy Carlson, Paul Hunter, Ace Moore, Paul Nelson, John and Roberta Olson, and others in the Red Sky Poetry Theatre orbit who commented helpfully on early drafts of these and other stories. Thanks to staff and fellow participants at the Community of Writers at Olympic Valley who commented helpfully on early drafts of these and other stories.

Stories from this collection have appeared in the following publications:
"Cindy's Tongue" in *Thieve's Jargon*
"Easy Money" in *Pindeldyboz*
"Mr. Big Mouth" in *Midnight Mind*
"Velcro & Zippers" in *The Raven Chronicles*

CONTENTS

VELCRO & ZIPPERS

A young man and a young woman sat in mismatched chairs at a card table in front of the window of the kitchen in their studio apartment. They were naked. A nub of white candle protruding from the neck of a wax-coated wine bottle on the table provided the only light. Despite the late hour, traffic roared by on the interstate two stories below.

The young man held the remnant of a joint to his lips with a roach-clip and positioned the lighter so that the flame grazed the end of it. He took a hit and handed the lighter and roach to the woman. He exhaled and watched her beautiful, moist lips form a tiny "O" around the end of the roach. The young woman raised her head and held the smoke in her lungs. She exhaled and set the roach on the ashtray.

"I was thinking, while we were making love, about Velcro," the young man said.

"Velcro," the woman said. "You were thinking about Velcro?"

"Yeah," the young man said. "See, one of your pubic hairs got wrapped around one of my pubic hairs, don't ask me how, but when I pulled back, it tugged."

She narrowed her eyes.

"*My* hair wrapped around *your* hair," she asked. She wagged a finger at him. "I'm sorry, but I think you mean one of *your* hairs wrapped around one of *my* hairs."

"Okay," he said. "One or the other. Our hairs wrapped around each other, one of mine and one of yours. They entwined."

She leaned forward. "But that's not what you said. You said *my* hair wrapped around *your* hair."

"Your point would be?" the man asked.

"My point is that my pubic hair did not grasp at your pubic hair. If anybody's hair was trying to

12

hold on, it would have been yours."

"Whatever," he said with a shrug. "Let me finish my story, okay? *Our* hairs embraced, and when I pulled back, it tugged."

"Yeah," she said. "So?"

"So, I thought to myself I thought, 'hey, that's like how Velcro works.' I was wondering if maybe that happened to the Velcro guy, the inventor, you know, Mr. Velcro."

"Velcro was invented by a woman," she said.

"No kidding?" he replied. "I didn't know that. So maybe it happened to her. Maybe Mr. Velcro was giving *Ms.* Velcro the business, and a pair of their pubic hairs entwined the way ours did."

"I have no idea who invented Velcro," she admitted. "But why did you assume it was a man?"

"I don't think I *assumed* anything. I simply said that maybe that is what happened to the *person* who invented Velcro."

"You said, *guy*," she corrected.

"Look, the shit was probably invented by a committee, okay? Men and women together. Why is everything an argument with you tonight?"

She turned and looked out the window. The sky was growing light, and traffic on the interstate was getting worse.

"Jesus," she said. "The sun is coming up."

"So pull the fuckin blinds down."

"I don't want to," she answered. "I want the people in the buildings across the interstate to see us sitting here naked as they prepare for work."

"Hey," the young man said. "Should this be the day we turn into grownups?"

"I thought we did that yesterday."

That had been the previous day's running gag, that they were going to suddenly change everything and turn into a couple from a '50s TV sitcom.

"Nope," he said. "We talked about it, but we never committed."

"I don't think today is such a good day for it,"

14

she said. "It looks like it's going to be awfully sunny out there."

The man reached over and yanked the cord. The blinds dropped and closed crookedly.

"Denial," the woman said.

"I would have to put my pants on soon if we were gonna turn into grownups," the young man said. "There'd be someplace important for me to go, probably."

"Do you think maybe it'll just happen," she asked. "We'll just wake up one morning and be grown-ups, like it or not?"

"Nope, no way. Not a chance in hell. We'll get old, that just happens. We could become parents, but being grown-ups, that's different. There is more to it."

"I'm still having a hard time understanding some of your distinctions," she said. "Anyhow, most of my friends have already metamorphosed. Or is it metamorphosized?"

"How the hell would I know?"

15

"Ginny has two kids," she continued. "I'm jealous of her, just like in sixth grade when she already had boobs, and I was still a flat-chested little girl. She's always ahead of me."

"Look at it this way, baby, you'll probably be dancin on her grave." He slapped a roach that was scampering across the table top. "Bad roach," he said, brushing it off his palm. "And anyhow, Ginny is not a grown-up. She is a wife and a mommy, but that does not make her a grown-up."

"But she's an adult, right?"

"Yeah, she's an adult."

"Maybe we should become adults, babe."

"Honey, we are adults! I thought I told you that. Didn't I tell you that?"

"I guess you did," she said. "But tell me once more. What, in your view, is the difference between an adult and a grown-up?"

"Oh, forget it. If you don't get it by now...." He picked up the roach-clip, held the roach to his lips, lit it and inhaled until it burned down to a minuscule twist of blackened paper. He dropped

16

the empty clip into the ashtray. "That's the end of that," he said. "We're gonna have to get some money."

"Do we have enough for the rent?" she asked.

"Yeah. And we got a week's worth of food."

"Well, then I guess we needn't worry," she said. She peered between the slats of the blinds at the cars rushing by below.

He looked at her beautiful face and breasts, her firm abdomen, all striped by bands of light and shadow, wondering what she was doing with him, why she had stayed as long as she had. He reached across the table and touched her cheek with his fingertips, then leaned forward and kissed her lips. He sat back. She smiled.

"Zippers," he said.

"Zippers?" she asked.

"Yeah, zippers. How do ya think zippers came about?"

EASY MONEY

I decide to stop for a drink at McWaverly's down in the west end of Long Beach on my way home from the job. This is back when I'm working as a baggage handler for Lufthansa out at Kennedy. Hadn't been to McWaverly's in years. Turns out my brother's old friend Mike D'Antonio is working the door.

"Little O'Mally," he says to me. "How's your brother?"

"He's all right," I say.

"I'm so bored, O'Mally," D'Antonio says. "Do me a favor, would ya? Start a fight. Just find the biggest guy in the place and pop him one."

"Nah," I say. "I ain't in the mood for fightin tonight."

"Alls ya gotta do is pop the chump once. I'll be

over to drag his ass out the door before he gets a mitt on ya."

"Nah, Mike," I say. "I'm tired. I just got off work."

"One punch," he says. "You're so tired ya can't throw one freakin punch? Remember the time I saved your ass from those Valley Stream punks?"

"Yeah, yeah," I say. "How many times have I paid ya back for that by now?"

"They pay me all right here, but no one ever fights. I never worked at such a chickenshit bar in my life. How come nobody fights? I'm gonna lose my edge if I don't practice." He reaches into the front pocket of his jeans and pulls out a ten. "Here, ten bucks," he says. He tries to stick the bill in my hand.

I shake my head *no* and hold up my palms.

"You drive a hard bargain, little O'Mally," he says. He reaches back into his pocket, takes out a twenty. He sets it atop the ten, folds them together, and slips the bills into my hand. "Thirty bucks, little O'Mally. Thirty goddamn bucks for one punch. I'm gonna fall asleep if I got nothin to do but check IDs all night. I just need an excuse to toss some guys around for a while. Go pop some chump so I can have a little fun, will ya?"

Every man's got his price, ain't that what they say? I pocket the thirty, wander into McWaverly's and look around for the biggest dude in the joint. There's a guy leaning on the bar down at the far end who's bigger than a brick shit-house, to use an overused expression that don't even make any damn sense. What the hell is a brick shit-house anyway? Anyhow, this guy, if you didn't know better, you'd swear he could tear D'Antonio to shreds from the looks of him. Plus, he's got a buddy with him who ain't exactly small either. Yeah, his buddy is probably the second or third biggest dude in the joint. They look tough enough to keep D'Antonio entertained for a while.

I weave my way through the crowd, stroll up and bump into the guy hard from behind. I throw my elbow into the back of his arm so the big glass mug he's holding swings up. His beer slops all over his shirt. He spins and gets in my face. I hit him once, hard as I can, with a right uppercut to the chin. It don't even phase him. My knuckles and wrist feel like I just punched a cinder block, but he don't look hurt at all, just mad.

I know I'm good as dead if I'm really fighting this guy myself but, sure enough, D'Antonio is on him quicker than him or his buddy can do me any damage. Soon as he grabs my shirt front with one hand and cocks the other fist back to knock my head off, D'Antonio gets between us. The crowd pulls back on all sides and forms a circle as the scuffle escalates into a beatdown.

D'Antonio proceeds to do what he does best. In no time he's in complete control. He's so damn fast you can't even make sense of what the hell he's doing half the time. A couple of punches, a pressure point hold, a Jiu Jitsu move, and both huge guys are falling all over the place with no idea what's happening to them. He sends the biggest guy careening one way and his buddy sprawling the other. They both get to their feet, furious, turn and charge to tackle him. He steps back at the perfect moment and lets them slam them face first into one another.

I don't stick around for the rest of the show. Seen it all before. I bolt for the door, head up the block, and climb into my Dodge Dart. I drive away to drink my easy money in another town. I sit outside at The Mermaid overlooking the canal in Freeport drinking my beer and wondering just how bad D'Antonio whomps them two chumps.

End of story? Don't I wish. A year-and-a-half, two years go by. I'm driving west on Sunrise Highway from my girlfriend's apartment in Merrick back to the animal house in Baldwin where I'm living with my cousin, a bunch of young, single city firemen, and a couple of bartenders. It's like three in the morning. I'm driving this heap of a Chevy Nova at the time. It's a real beater, but I got ideas about muscling it up if I can scrape the cash together. All of a sudden she goes tits up on me right in the middle of the highway. The engine coughs and she conks out.

I coast to the side of the road, put the flashers on, pop the hood and start nosing around trying to figure out what's what. A guy stops, pulls a uey, and noses his red Ford Mustang up bumper to bumper with me. He steps out holding a set of jumper cables and walks toward me. He's huge. There's something familiar about the guy, but I can't place him right off. He recognizes me, though. When I see the anger in his eyes, that's when I remember where I saw him before. He hits me so hard my knees buckle and my feet flop up off the ground before the back of my head cracks down on the curb.

Can you imagine how it feels when the swirling stars and fog clear from your mind, and you find yourself curled into a ball beside the highway with a broken nose, bleeding from the back of your head, hoping for mercy, thinking, *God, oh dear God, I deserve this,* as a giant of a man, a fine, decent giant of a man, who stops in the middle of the night to help a stranger, whips you again and again with the sharp metal clips of his jumper cables?

HOW FRANK MET FRANKIE

I walk into that dump in East Rockaway. You know the place, that old man bar. Who should I see sitting there but who's-his-face's ex old lady, what's-her-name.

"You!" I say, like I'm all surprised, 'cause I am.

"Lenny!" she says. "It's been freakin ages!"

"Frank," I say.

"That's right," she says. "Lenny was that buddy of yours."

"I don't know any Lenny," I say.

"Whatever," she says and shrugs. And she's exactly right. Whatever.

"So what's a pretty thing like you doin in a dump like this," I say.

"There's a new line," she says. She raises her

bottle and smirks. "Take a wild fuckin guess, eh?" She throws her head back, slams her beer, then leans across the bar so her rack is halfway hanging out the top of her halter. "Joe-Joe, honey-baby!" she sings. "Be a love, eh?"

Joe-Joe, more likely Joe, sneers. He's a young, handsome twerp, the sort you'd look for an excuse to beat the crap out of just for jealousy. Now I know what she's doing here. She ain't got a chance in hell, I can see that. So I sidle up on the stool beside her figuring I can snatch up Joe-Joe's scraps around closing time. Hell, what's-her-name ain't the worst looking woman in the world. Not by a long shot. A good looking young guy like Joe-Joe ain't gonna give her the time of day, but for a regular looking mug like me, who maybe isn't quite over the hill yet but is getting damn near the top of it, she's a catch.

"So what are *you* doin here," she asks.

"Wanted to have a drink someplace I'm not likely to see old faces," I say. "But I walk in and the first face I see--"

"Yeah," she says and laughs. She points at herself and makes a funny face. She glances around at the trembling old, drooling men who call the place home. "Nothin *but* old faces in this joint," she says.

"Tell me about it. It's a zombie convention."

"Night of the Livin Dead," she says. "Except you, Joe-Joe, baby!" She about lunges over the bar, she leans so far forward. "You're a doll! Ain't you my doll-boy, baby?"

One old guy with his eyes bugged out and his mostly toothless mouth gaping open like he'd seen some dude's head explode in World War I or, shit, maybe the Civil War, and never got over it, goes shuffling by on feet he is apparently incapable of lifting more than a tenth of an inch off the floor. There's ghosts younger than this guy. Yeah, *there are,* whatever. Get off my back about the goddamn grammar, just let me tell ya the story. You couldn't look at the man without thinking he was a warning that some life-threatening horror was waiting behind the very next door you open.

Joe-Joe sets what's-her-name's new beer down, snatches up a few bills and scampers back to the cash register before she can get ahold of him. Poor kid. Grandson of one of these sorry-ass old regulars, I suspect, putting in his time at this dump to get the experience so he can get a gig in a decent pub.

"Take your tip, honey!" She grabs a fistful of bills. "Come on let me stuff your pockets, ha-ha!"

He shakes his head, red-faced and smiling, and stays near the register. He scans the old farts 'til he finds one needing a refill.

"Take it," she says, pitching the bills to flutter and drop to the sticky rubber mat behind the bar.

Truth be told, I was looking to have a quiet pitcher or two alone. I was thinking maybe I had to quit drinking, maybe get into rehab, something like that. Anytime I got heavy thinking to do, I like to find a quiet place to sit and drink alone.

Thing was, the weekend before, I woke up in the backseat of my Impala early one morning parked next to a dumpster behind a 7-11 in

Rockaway Beach not knowing where I'd been or even, for the first few minutes, who I was. Dried puke all over my shirt. Couldn't account for the past two days. That shit scared me. Was a trembling mess for nearly a week easing my way out of it with shots of Wild Turkey every few hours. Lost my job, of course. Boss left a nice message on the machine the first day but was cursing me out by the end of the week saying how I had one more day to get to the job site and claim my tools or he'd sell them to the pawn shop since I screwed him in the middle of this big project.

But now I was feeling better and things were looking up, what with my running into what's-her-name while she's all worked up about this kid Joe-Joe who ain't gonna give her the time of day. Figured I could talk my way into a one-nighter and postpone the brooding session for a while.

So, long story short; yak, yak, yak, coins in the jukebox, singing along to the oldies, yak, yak some more, shots and beers. Closing time approaches and she figures out she ain't getting what she's dreaming of. I make my move, wrap my arm around her waist, snuggle my nose into her hair, lips to her ear, and whisper, "ah, hell, baby, that little twerp wouldn't know what to do with a woman like you anyhow. He's intimidated by you, girl. Now, whyn't you come on home with a man who appreciates and knows how to treat a lady?"

She smiles. "Sounds like fun. I used to think about that once in a while, Lenny. Me and you gettin together."

"Frank," I say.

"Yeah, Frank," she says. "You and Lenny both. I used to imagine it with the both of you. Like a three-way, ya know?"

I still have no idea who the fuck Lenny is and the idea of having some other dude there butt-ass naked while I'm trying to stick it to some chick is too much of a freak-out for me to ever even consider, but all I say is, "yeah?"

"Ooh, yeah," she goes. "If I hadn't been steady with--"

"Yeah, you and who's-his-face--"

"Exactly. Hey, I ain't had quite enough nightlife yet."

"No?"

"I know this after-hours place."

"Yeah?"

"It's lots of fun," she says.

"Sure you wouldn't wanna--"

"Oh, yeah," she says. "Sure, baby, sure. But what's the rush? Another drink first."

"Okay. Sure. What the hell," I say.

"You got a car?"

"Right out back," I say. I toss a couple of bills on the bar and lead the way out.

The Impala starts on the third try.

"What junkyard did you yank this hunk of crap outta," she asks.

"It's a classic," I say.

"It's a piece of shit."

"It's a classic piece of shit."

I back out, drive up the alley and onto the main drag.

"So where is this place," I ask.

"Queens."

"Okay, Queens. Where in Queens?"

"Whataya mean, where in Queens? It's in Queens!"

"Queens is a big place," I say. "I mean, where we goin, Flushing, Howard Beach, Long Island City, Astoria?"

"I don't know what town. I know where it is, okay? Just drive."

"Just drive?"

"Just drive! Get on the Belt Parkway and head west. Can ya do that? Can you find the fuckin Belt Parkway for fuck sake or do I have to--"

"I know how to get to the goddamn Belt, duh! Of course I do."

"Well, great! Do that, then. Get on the fuckin Belt and I'll, ya know, point ya left, right and all that shit when we get close."

I shake my head. She's all quiet and pouty and looking out the window and fidgeting with the radio knobs while I drive us to the Belt Parkway and head west for who knows where in Queens. She won't settle on a song for more than five seconds before she's twisting the knob again looking for something else. Finally, she settles on a classic rock station and starts talking again, accompanied by the Stones playing "Wild Horses."

"He's never gonna fuck me," she says.

"Huh?"

"That little faggot."

"Joe-Joe?"

"That good lookin, he's gotta be a faggot."

"Aw, hell, baby. He's probably got the girls crawlin all over him. Probably gettin all he can handle with gals his own age."

"Faggot."

"Leave him be."

"Meant you that time."

"Hey!"

"Stickin up for him 'cause you got the hots for him."

"Stop."

"You're more into him than I am."

"Knock it off!"

"Oughta have his face right here, the way I tip the little prick," she says spreading her blue-jeaned thighs wide on the seat and grabbing hold of herself with both hands right in close to the sweet spot. "For fuck sake, drive on the right side of the road!" she shouts.

I veer back across the double yellows as horns blare all around.

"Well, shit, if you're gonna distract me like that," I explain. "And then it's all my fault when--"

"Look out!"

I veer and swerve.

"That's our exit!"

I accelerate then brake and somehow make it onto the off-ramp without killing anybody.

"Okay, straight up this way awhile," she says.

"Seriously?"

"Yeah, it's right around here somewhere."

"Baby, ain't nothin's right around here."

"I'm tellin ya, it's -- okay turn right at this corner."

I make a right. The dirty old brick buildings are mostly boarded up on the ground floor. You can see, through the broken windows of the upper floors, that the insides of most of them had been gutted by fire. Nobody's paying rent in them, that's for sure, but there's people walking the streets, guys who look like crack zombies mostly, so I figure the buildings are full of squatters.

"Okay, left," she says.

I make the next left. There are old wrecks of cars without wheels along the curb that people are living in.

"What the fuck kinda neighborhood is this?"

"Duh! It's a shitty neighborhood, dumbass! I told ya it was an after-hours club! After-hours clubs are *illegal*. Where the fuck did you think it would be? South fuckin Hampton? Beverly motherfuckin Hills, Califuckinfornia, dipshit?"

"All right, all right, enough with the hostility already! Shit! I'm just a little nervous, okay? My tabs are expired, I got no insurance, I don't know where the fuck we are and--"

She shakes her head. "Well, this is great. This is just fuckin great. You're such a goddamn – oh, hey, there it is!"

"Where?"

"Right there! Find a spot."

I look where she's pointing. Just another burnt-out building with plywood across the first floor, but there's a giant standing there with his arms crossed. And I do mean a giant. Seven-foot plus and an extra-huge head and enormous hands like from that disease I saw on a documentary on TV, the one that pro wrestler dude had, where their shit never stops growing.

She jumps out soon as I park and runs that ridiculous girl-in-high-heels run that's so sexy when the young ones do it but embarrassing to see an older gal with a full womanly ass like what's-her-name do. I get out quick and hurry to catch up.

"Tiny!" she shouts up at the giant. She hugs his waist.

"Darlin," Tiny says. He sets his enormous palms on her shoulders, puckers up and gives her a kiss on top of the head. He opens the makeshift plywood door and waves her through. I take a step forward but Tiny halts me with a massive palm on my chest.

"Twenty dollars."

"I'm with her."

"Okay, you're with her. That means we'll let you in. For twenty dollars."

"But--"

He slides that enormous paw up to my neck and gives a suggestive squeeze. "Twenty dollars."

I pay the man. He opens the door, gives a slight bow and waves me in.

The floor inside is concrete. There's a disco ball hanging from the ceiling and a DJ set up against the back wall. He's spinning Saturday Night Fever era disco like it's still 1978 even though the goddamn Eighties are nearly over. The bar is on the left. What's-her-name is standing beside the last booth against the right wall. A man with a black mustache stands and kisses her. He's dressed in an expensive looking, ugly gray suit with a maroon shirt but no tie. I look around. Everyone is dressed pretty nice – slacks, expensive looking shoes, dress shirts. I feel like a dirtbag in my jeans, workboots, denim jacket. And what's worse, half the guys in the place are glaring at me.

Someone behind me asks his buddy, "who the fuck is that," real fast like it's one word, *"whoduhfuckizat?"*

I don't look back.

"Never seen him before," his buddy says.

The place is obviously not just an illegal after-hours joint, it's some kind of private club, and I'm definitely not a member.

The guy with the mustache and what's-her-name sit down in the booth. I walk over hesitantly, thinking it'd probably be smarter to turn right around, ditch what's-her-name, and leave. The first thing I notice is that the table top is a mirror. The second thing I notice is the white pile of coke in the middle of it. The third thing I notice, when the guy sees me and reaches for it, is the handgun.

What's-her-name, who's sitting beside the man, looks up and frowns.

"You brought him?" the man asks her.

"I needed a ride, Frankie. My car's on the fritz. I figured he'd get the hint when I ran for it, but he followed me. I guess Tiny thought we was together."

"He's all right," the man with the mustache, the man I've just learned is named Frankie, asks what's-her-name.

43

"He's okay. He'll be no trouble. You've got my word." She gestures to him then to me. "Frankie," she says, "this is Lenny. I mean Frank. Oh, look at that! Frankie and Frank."

"Hello Frank," Frankie says. "Sit." He nods to the seat across the table from them. I sit. Frankie offers his hand. I shake the sweaty thing.

"And how do you know Babydoll, Frank?" he asks me, nodding to whats-her-name.

"Oh, here and there. Bars and pubs and parties."

"He was on the same bowling team with my ex-boyfriend," Babydoll says.

"Softball," I correct.

"That's right, softball. It was Lenny was on the bowling team."

"That's nice. That's very nice." Frankie smiles a weird, dreamy smile that makes me uncomfortable. I got the impression that he was imagining himself strangling me.

"Whataya carry?"

44

"Huh?"

He grabs the gun, holds it up so I can see it. "Your piece," he says. "Whataya carry?"

"Me? Uh... shit, man. Nothin." I grin and shrug.

"No gun?" He turns and smiles at Babydoll.

She shrugs and looks away.

"He's a citizen, Babydoll? He's a *citizen* and you bring him here? He's got no connections to any of us, and you bring him here?"

"It's like I told ya, Frankie, I needed a ride. I thought there's no way he's followin me in here. Only a total moron wouldn't see what's what and take the hint, right?"

Frankie looks at me. "You're a good boy, eh? No gun? A good boy. Like a little baby in shorts sucking a lollipop, eh?"

He slaps my cheek lightly and laughs. Then I laugh. What's-her-name laughs. We all three laugh our very different lonely laughs together.

Frankie rocks his forearm on the pivot of his elbow, shakes the weapon, which appears to be some kind of automatic, though I don't know jack squat about guns. I know it's not a revolver. Like any other dumbass who's ever seen a cowboy movie, I know what those look like. Frankie's gun was more square looking. The handle and the barrel were more rectangular than rounded, and the bullets were loaded by a clip through the base of the handle.

"This gun, it's fully automatic," Frankie says. "Squeeze the trigger once and hold, it keeps shooting 'til you let go or run outta bullets." He turns it side to side and admires it. "With Teflon bullets and this gun, you can kill an elephant hiding behind a rhinoceros inside a fuckin tank." He smiles.

I nod and whistle my approval.

"You believe me, Frank?"

"Yeah."

"Do you believe me?"

"I do."

He stares directly into my eyes, leans across the table getting as close to my face as he can without standing.

"Do you, Frank? Do you believe me?"

"I do, Frankie. I believe you."

He stares until I look away. He holds the gun out to me, flat on his palm like he wants me to take it from him, hold it, get a feel for it, so I reach for it. He snatches it back with one quick movement, aims it at my face.

"Bang, bang, bang!" he says. He laughs. He looks at Babydoll and jerks the gun three times like he's firing it into my face and says, "bang, bang, bang!"

We all laugh our lonely, solitary laughs together again.

Frankie sets the pistol down and turns to Babydoll. "This ain't the shit we sell the punks, Babydoll," he says. He glares at me, picks the gun up off the mirror-topped table, and holsters it under his arm inside his suit jacket. He shovels some coke loose from the pile with a razor and cuts a few lines. "This is the good shit. Pure. This is the friends-and-family shit."

He takes a Benjamin from his pocket, rolls it up and slips it into a small gold tube to hold it in place. He hands it to her. She snorts a line, switches nostrils, does another. Frankie passes the rolled bill to me. I lower my head to the table and snort two lines. He's telling the truth about the purity. It doesn't burn my nostrils. I realize it's probably the first time I'd snorted coke that wasn't mixed with speed and baby powder and who knows what the fuck else goes into the crap chumps like me get sold by dealers looking to up their profits. I gaze around at all the fancy suits and nice dresses.

It's hard to figure how exactly Babydoll fits in with this world. Now that I'm thinking of her as Babydoll, it's bugging me that I can't remember what the hell her real name is... or was. Who knows, maybe the name I knew her by back in the day – Barbara Ann? Mary Ann? Carrie Ann? – wasn't her real name either.

It's not like I really knew her. Her ex was a teammate, a friend of a friend of an acquaintance, another loser like me who wanted to be on a summer softball team in his forties. It's not like we were a bunch of guys who grew up together, that summer's team.

"I've got a friend for you to meet, Babydoll," Frankie says to her. "He'll be good for you."

She rubs her fingers and thumb together. "Good, Frankie? How good, eh? Ya know what I'm sayin? How good?" She laughs possibly the ugliest laugh I've ever heard.

"Very good, baby. Very good." He smiles like an angry child delightedly torturing a kitten.

"I'm game," she says and laughs again.

"Yes. Yes, you are," Frankie answers. "Tony!" he yells.

A large ugly man I hadn't seen before is standing beside the booth all of a sudden. He must've been hovering right nearby in the shadows all along.

"Tony, you can be done for the night, eh? You done good today. Damn good. Angelo, Sonny, and Eddie are still around. We got Tiny at the door. All is cool. You know Babydoll, eh? You seen her

49

around, right?"

Tony smiles and nods.

"She's a good lady," Frankie says. "So you two, you go have fun for a few days, eh? Take a trip down to Atlantic City or whatever and live a little."

He reaches into his jacket pocket and draws out a roll of bills. He licks his thumb and counts out a bunch of hundreds with the quick ease of a man who's comfortable around money. He slaps the stack down on the edge of the table.

"Here's for today." He counts out a bunch more and sets a second stack perpendicular on top of the first. "Here's for whatever." He counts out a third stack. "And this is for the lady." He smiles at Babydoll but puts the bills on Tony's pile. Tony scoops up the money and stuffs it into his jacket pocket.

"All right, let's go, Babydoll," Tony says. "Let's hit the road."

Babydoll gets up and struts away hand-in-hand with big, ugly Tony. She don't so much as nod goodbye. So there I am sitting in the booth with Frankie. Just me and him. But we're not alone for long. Tony stops to talk with some guys on his way out. Three of them walk over and nod to Frankie. He nods in return. The three men stand there in military style "at ease" posture, hands held together behind their backs. None of them speak. They simply stand there silently glaring at me while Frankie speaks.

"Frank," he says. "Frank, Frank, Frank." He smiles and glares all at once.

It starts in my toes, the shiver, and rattles my whole terrified body right up to the top of my head.

"You're friends with her, eh," Frankie asks me. "With Babydoll?"

"Yeah, uh-huh. Friends. Just friends!" I hold up my palms for emphasis. I laugh to show I'm relaxed. But I'm not. It's a lie, the attempt at a casual laugh. Instead of the calm, manly chuckle I was aiming for, it comes out as a high-pitched hysterical titter verging on a whimpering whine.

51

"Just friends, huh," Frankie says. "That's good. It's good to have friends, right?"

"Oh, yeah," I agree. "Gotta have friends."

"Friends are important," Frankie says. He reaches across the table and pats my wrist, then gives it a squeeze, then clamps down on it like a vice. "Friends," he says. "You gotta have somebody watchin your back, right? A man's got no friends, he's got nothin. All the money in the world won't do ya no good without friends." He glances at the three men standing beside the booth. "This club is full of friends, Frank. Most men here would kill for me and many would die for me, understand? Anyone who is not a good friend does not last long here. Fake friends, or stupid friends, or friends who talk too much disappear. They just disappear, Frank. Do you understand?"

"I understand."

"Do you?"

"I do."

"Do you really?" He reaches into his suit jacket

and retrieves the automatic from his holster. He aims it at my face, leans forward, and does the staring match routine again.

"I really, really do."

"Good. Give me your driver's license."

"Why?"

"Because I told you to. And I'm holding a gun. And you're not. And we're in my club surrounded by my friends, not in your club surrounded by your friends."

I dig out my wallet, take out the license, and pass it to him with my shaking hand.

"Okay Frank Henderson of 237 Pierce Avenue, Apartment # 3, Rockland Park, New York," he says. "I'm gonna keep this. If it seems there's pigs who aren't tight with us snoopin around more than usual like someone's been talkin, I'll have some friends visit and make sure some noisy someone is made into a nice, quiet corpse. If you move, I'll have my friends on the police force find your new address for me. Do we understand each other?"

"Yes we do."

"Do we?"

"We do."

"Do we really?"

"We really, really, really do."

"Okay, Frank. I believe you. Get the fuck outta here."

I stand. I look at the three men lined up beside the booth. The three men look at Frankie. Frankie nods. The three men step back and make room for me to pass. I make a B-line for the door quick as I can walk without breaking into a run, hoping no one's got any reason to stop me.

I slide out past Tiny onto the street and run to my car. I can't get the keys out of my pocket because I'm trembling. I finally manage to get them out and get the door open. My hand is shaking all over the place. I have to hold my trembling right wrist with my trembling left hand to get the key into the ignition. I'm looking in the rearview hoping not to see anyone coming up behind me. The engine coughs and belches and finally turns over. I drive away in search of the

Belt Parkway East, then things get blurry. The coke and panic-induced adrenaline rush perked me up awhile but was no match for all the booze I drank before and oncoming exhaustion.

I come to in the back of the Impala and sit up. Daylight. I'm beside the dumpster in a Dunkin Donuts parking lot. Which Dunkin Donuts in what town? Who the hell knows. Who cares. I'm alive. Things could be worse. Things could be much worse. I open the door and crawl out onto the asphalt. The blood is pounding in my head. My mouth is dry and tastes like an old sock. I stand, holding myself steady with the roof of the car. I stuff my free hand into a pocket and find I've got some cash left. Yeah, things could be much worse. I stagger across the parking lot toward the first cup of coffee and doughnut of the rest of my life.

MR. BIG MOUTH

I let him do all the talking. You know how he could talk and talk.

"It coulda been any one of us," he says. "That's all I'm saying."

I nod. I don't say nothing until right at the end. I'm all smiles, buying the drinks like everything is fine. Two old pals.

"It coulda even been you or me, eh," he says. "Nobody likes having a big mouth around, especially at a place like this."

He gulps beer from his bottle, ashes his cigarette into the tar-blackened glass tray.

"We're all people who know people," he says. "Know what I'm sayin? When you're around people who know people, ya gotta hold your tongue. That's what I'm sayin. Me, I know how to hold my tongue. No one's gonna find me face down in the parkin lot with a bullet in my head or floatin around in the marsh behind Kennedy Airport. No siree."

Horowitz and two of the others are on stools at the bar. Smiley's on the business side of it, of course, chewing their ears about something. Pastorelli and a couple of fellas are sitting at a table nearby. Schmidt is by himself leaning on the end of the bar.

I remember I notice the cigarette smoke, that there's so much of it swirling around the lamps hanging from the ceiling that you'd think the place is on fire. You know those lamps there with the shades like them hats Chinamen wear when they're picking rice? In the movies? You know how them lamps sway around from the air conditioner vent?

Two guys are playing a lazy game of pool like they just need something to do while they work out their plan. You can tell there's no money on the game. Everyone else in the place is okay, but we gotta wait 'til the pool players are gone.

Nothing can happen 'til they clear out.

He takes a drag on the cigarette and looks around the room. He nods toward the table where Pastorelli and them are sitting.

"Take our boy Pastorelli over there," he whispers. "Pretty big boy in the Teamsters and, as you know, has arrangements with a certain prominent member of a certain important family who shall remain nameless. Guy like that, he don't want no blabbermouth around, ya know? Just on principle. Not even for any special reason just, whataya call it, preventive maintenance, capiche? Eliminate the problem before it can occur. I'm not sayin he did it or had it done. I'm just sayin coulda been, that's all. Coulda been. Me, I don't know nothin, I don't wanna know nothin. I can talk with you about these things, we go way back, but I don't peep a word to nobody else. Nobody."

He nods toward Schmidt.

"Or take our boy Schmidt there," he says. "Good man, Officer Schmidt, and a good cop, I'm sure, but he likes his nose candy. Don't make him a bad person. Don't even make him a bad cop 'cause he's got discretion, see? City cop at home on Long Island, off-duty, after hours, out of uniform having a drink or two at the bar like anybody would. Okay, so he steps into the back for a little tootsky now and again, so what? He's not in his jurisdiction. It's nobody's business. Hell, maybe he even makes a little coin on the side with it, eh? A little supplementary income from on-the-job drug seizures, perhaps? Yeah, maybe not all the evidence gets turned in, know what I'm sayin? What's the problem with it? There ain't no problem until some fat mouth starts talkin.

"I ain't sayin it was Schmidt; I'm only sayin it coulda been. Me, I don't inquire about what I shouldn't know, and I don't blab what I do. That's why I'm sittin here enjoyin a nice cold beer on a summer night while Mr. Big Mouth is feedin worms."

He drank a gulp of beer.

"And then there's Horowitz over there. He's a

fuckin cucumber, Horowitz. Cool as ice. You could watch his face all day and not once guess what he's thinkin. Tell me Horowitz wouldn't have his reasons for wantin to see Mr. Big Mouth face down in the dirt with a bullet in his head. You know Mr. Big Mouth with his opinions, 'the Jews this and the Jews that.' Got fuckin sick and tired of hearin it myself and I ain't even a Jew. Plus Horowitz, bein so professional and cool and uncatchable and wantin to keep it that way, if anybody don't want a big mouth around it's Horowitz.

"Remember he was makin some of his coin on the water, Mr. Big Mouth? Swipin depth-finders and radios and so forth off yachts? He comes in here blabbin to everyone how he's makin a fortune raidin the Israeli Navy of Bagel Beach. Big fuckin joke, right? A guy that quick to shoot his mouth off about his own operation ain't gonna think twice about blabbin on somebody else, right? Yeah, it coulda been Horowitz did him in. Ain't sayin it was, just sayin it coulda been. Okay, who knows, maybe it really was that black kid they picked up, but I doubt it. The more I think about it, the more I see how easy it would be to off a guy like Mr. Big Mouth. Way I see it, it was someone he knew, someone who thought he knew too much and was talkin too much and needed to be shut up good. So, he's walkin across the lot at four, four thirty in the mornin, shit-face drunk and last to leave as always. Blammo! Someone tags him quick and sweet in the back of the skull, takes the wallet just for show, and that's that. No more Mr. Big Mouth to worry about. I'm glad it's been done, whoever did it. Fuck him. It's his own damn fault, not knowin when to shut up. He's dead and the world's a better place without him."

The two fellas playing pool finish their game. They pay up and throw a tip on the bar and walk out. It's only all of us in there now.

That's when I talk.

"You're a pretty bright boy," I say.

"What's that?" he says.

Schmidt walks over and latches the door. Pastorelli and the fellas stand up. Horowitz and them spin on their stools and stand.

"I says, you're a pretty bright boy. You're pretty good at figurin things out, ain't ya?"

"I guess you could say that," he says. "I guess you could say I'm a pretty bright boy."

"Nah," I say. "You ain't too bright. You ain't too bright at all... Mr. Big Mouth."

You shoulda seen the look on his face. You shoulda seen his face when he saw what was coming.

PROGRESS ON

THE P FIVER

Angie and Patty sat side by side in their usual spot on the smokers' bench about a hundred yards east of the front entrance of the Zinzertech Enterprises building. They were bundled in their parkas against the late autumn chill. Angie cupped one hand around her cigarette and flicked the lighter with the other. She took a drag, blew the smoke out the right side of her mouth, and handed the lighter to Patty.

"So what are we, the last two smokers in all of Elmwood Hills Office Park, or what," Angie asked.

"Are you kiddin, Angie," Patty said. "We're the last two smokers on all of Long Island!" She took a puff, exhaled, then hugged herself and shivered.

"Sometimes it seems like it," Angie agreed.

"Last real, unrepentant smokers," Patty said.

"Right? Everybody's on the patch."

"Quitters."

"Not me."

"Same here, girl," Patty said. "I'm a lifer. I love these damn things. They'll be the death of us, these damn ciggies, but I love 'em."

Angie took a drag then held her cigarette up in front of her face and shook it. "Maybe if I ever get out of this nut-house I can think about quittin the smokes, but right now my cigs are all that are holdin me together. I'm tellin ya, Patty, I can't take much more."

"Believe me, I know," Patty said. "Don't tell a soul, but I'm polishin up my rezzie."

"No!"

"Don't tell a soul!"

"You're my idol."

"Do it, Angie. Get the rezzie out and start job

70

huntin. Get out of this nut-house before you turn into one of the crazies. I mean, did you see Eddie Michaelson yesterday?"

"Oh, poor Eddie," Angie said. "The stress he's under. Yeah, that man is headed for the rubber room if he doesn't get outta here soon. He didn't come in this mornin."

"Really?"

"Not a sign of him. The guy's blood pressure has to be off the chart. His face looks like a tomato half the time." Angie hugged herself and bounced her feet up and down as if running in place. "So here's my mornin," she said. "Off to a hell of a start. Bob sticks his head into my cubicle and asks, 'how's progress on the P540A/107GN2-J?'"

"Oh God, the P-fiver." Patty shook her head and frowned. "I am so sick of the P-fiver."

"Tell me about it. The only thing I'm sicker of than the P540A/107GN2-J is hearin it called the P-fiver. No offense to you, Patty."

Patty turned her head and sneered, but said

nothing.

"Anyhoo," Angie continued, "I'm like, 'progress on the P540A/107GN2-J? *What progress* on the P540A/107GN2-J? Haven't you heard? Engineerin hit a roadblock on the P540A/107GN2-J. We've all been workin on the Z910L/304TN3-K."

"Yeah, right?" Patty said. "Everybody's workin on the Z-niner now. What's the story with that guy?"

"He's outta the loop," Angie said. "He thinks he's totally in the loop but he's out of it. He's always two steps behind the real inner-loopers. The only thing I'll say for him, though, is he's a full-name-of-the-part man. None of that Z-niner crap for Bob. No offense to you. Anyhoo, he gives me this look. You know his look? That smug Bob face of his?"

"Oh, I know it, yeah. I totally know the look." Patty turned toward Angie, smiled and squinched her nose in imitation of Bob's smug look.

"That's exactly it, Patty. That's the face.

'Haven't *you heard*,' he says to me, all snotty like that. 'The P540A/107GN2-J roadblock's been cleared. Engineerin's back on track with the P540A/107GN2-J. What's more, they've hit a new snafu with the Z910L/304TN3-K. Progress on the Z910L/304TN3-K is on hold until they determine the workaround.'"

"It'll drive you crazy if you let it."

"Drive me? Too late to drive me crazy, Patty. I've been driven all the way there and let out at the curb. I'm kookoo, I swear. Certifiable." Angie stubbed her cigarette and checked her watch. "Time for one more," she said. She shook another cig from the pack and lit up.

"One more? Nah, we're havin two more, Angie. To hell with them. Let anybody say anythin if we walk in a few minutes late, I swear. Maybe if we go back in late enough we'll get lucky, and they'll fire us on the spot."

"Oh, if there's a God in heaven, Patty. If there's a God in heaven." Angie took another drag off her second cigarette. "But that's just the start of it. So,

73

okay, the Z910L/304TN3-K paperwork goes back into folders, back into the drawer, right? I'm workin away on the P540A/107GN2-J when Lenny comes by and goes, 'how's that Z910L/304TN3-K comin along?' I'm like, 'what! Bob just told me the Z910L/304TN3-K is on hold. I've gone back to work on the P540A/107GN2-J. 'Bob?' he says. 'Since when does anyone listen to Bob?'"

"Well, he's got a point there, Angie. You gotta admit."

"Don't rub it in. He goes, 'the P540A/107GN2-J is a goner, kaput, dead in the water. Haven't you heard? It's a no-go with the P540A/107GN2-J. We're full steam ahead with the Z910L/304TN3-K. I need that paperwork! Get me the Z910L/304TN3-K paperwork pronto!' he says. 'I need it the day before yesterday!' he says."

"They plan it, Angie. I swear they do. In their little closed-door meetins, that's what the do. 'How can we make Patty crazy this week? Angie doesn't look stressed enough. What can we do to make her miserable? And let's send Darlene right around the bend tomorrow.'"

"It wouldn't surprise me in the least to find out it's the God's honest truth, Patty. I swear it wouldn't."

"Oh, and you think we're on the verge, huh? You think we're half an inch from losin it? Look who's comin."

Red-faced Eddie Michaelson strode up the sidewalk. He swung his briefcase back and forth at his side and pulled a rolling suitcase behind him with the other hand.

"My God, is his heart gonna just explode or what?"

"His brain, Patty. His brain's gonna explode. Just look at that face. Look at that red, red face. His head is so full of angry blood."

"Polish up the rezzie, girl. Get outta here. I'm takin the first offer I get. Anywhere's better than here."

Michaelson glanced at them and paused and turned slightly as if he was thinking about coming over to talk with them. He turned his head left and looked at the Zinzertech Enterprises building entrance. He turned his head right and looked at Angie and Patty. Angie and Patty waved. Michaelson nodded and continued on his way toward the building entrance.

"Why's he got the suitcase," Angie asked. "He's not goin on the California trip, is he?"

"No, I think they all left yesterday, didn't they?"

"Maybe he's a last minute add, and he's pickin up some things and flyin out to meet them this afternoon."

"Stranger things have happened."

"Well, shall we mosey back in?"

"Nah, I wasn't kiddin, Angie. I'm smokin a third. I'm sittin right here and takin a half-hour break and smokin a third cigarette, and if anyone in there has any problem with it, they can kiss my ass."

Angie laughed. "I don't know what I'd do without you, Patty. Yeah, I'm with you, girl." She lit a third cigarette, inhaled and let the smoke curl out of her nose and lips. She and Patty sat in silence enjoying their small act of rebellion.

"What is that," Patty asked.

"What's what?"

Patty placed her palm on Angie's arm. "That. Don't you hear that?"

"What?"

"That."

"What?"

"That." She held her pointer finger up beside her face.

Angie tilted her head and focused all her attention on listening. She heard it.

Pop! Pop-pop-pop-pop! Pop-pop! Pop-pop-pop-pop!

She widened her eyes and let her mouth drop open. She turned toward Patty. She wrapped her arms around her friend.

"Oh, my God...."

"No," Patty said before Angie even asked the

question. She shook her head. "No, it couldn't be. It just couldn't. No, no, no, no, no, no, no."

The popping sounds continued. They looked toward the Zinzertech Enterprises building. A tall window in the second floor conference room shattered, and a long table dropped to the lawn. They watched as the group of their coworkers who'd rammed it against the glass leapt down, scrambled to their feet and ran.

LAUGHTER, PATHOS & MUSCLES

I found out this evening that my boyhood friend, Jimmy Willis, was killed in a pileup on Interstate 80. He was driving home from a business trip when a tractor-trailer truck jackknifed ahead of him. I am looking now at a picture of his son and two daughters, these suddenly fatherless children, whom I've never met. Jimmy and I exchanged Christmas cards for a few years, so I have this picture, three smiling little blond kids sprawled on a big lawn, their faces flushed from play, who've obviously been corralled by adults to sit still a moment. Their eyes are full of mischief, and they look ready to spring back into action as soon as they get the word. The boy, ten or eleven years old, is the image of his father at that age.

I hadn't seen Jimmy in years, but there was a

time when he and I were partners and believed that a day would come when the names McDougal and Willis would be known and loved around the world. At the public school on Long Island where Jimmy and I met, there was a custodian who we all called Muscles on account of the size of his arms. His biceps would have been impressive on a man of any age. Since he was well into his sixties, they were all the more impressive. Sometimes you'd see Muscles with a bemused look on his face, rubbing the gray stubble atop his head and muttering under his breath. He would go striding bowlegged down the hallway, swinging his big, tattooed arms, and whistling out the side of his mouth. Every so often, he'd stop dead in his tracks, wink and shoot a kid with his finger.

When his work happened to lead him through the cafeteria during lunch-time, tables of boys and girls would shout, "hey, Muscles, show us your muscles!" He'd oblige us and weave among the tables flexing his arms, making crazy faces, and rattling off one-liners. Even the crabby, old lunch ladies had to laugh when Muscles put on a show. When he was in an especially good mood, he'd add the much loved grand finale to his act. He'd pop out his dentures, hold them between fingers and thumb and, with his lips wrapped in over his empty gums, do a ventriloquist routine trying his damnedest not to move his jaw.

No one appreciated this more than Jimmy Willis and I. We were both huge comedy fans. After school every weekday, we'd watch the Three Stooges, I Love Lucy, and The Honeymooners. We both spent our Saturday afternoons in front of TV, too, watching the movies of Abbott and Costello, Laurel and Hardy, and the Bowery Boys.

During recess, while other kids were playing touch football or swinging on the swings, Jimmy and I were imitating the slaps, bonks, trips, and pratfalls or our comedy heroes. We got good enough that we attracted an audience of kids who'd sit around the sandbox while we spouted a jumbled, "who's on first...why I oughta...sorry, Ollie...," dialogue of stolen lines.

One afternoon, Jimmy and I were in the cafeteria eating our lunches with a bunch of other little jokers when Jimmy said, "hey, Eddie, look!" He screwed up his eyes like Curly, said, "whoop, whoop, whoop!" and threw a banana peel over his shoulder. I chuckled, knowing that if we were in a comedy movie and not real life someone would come along step on it and go flying in the air. As Jimmy stood to go retrieve the peel, Muscles came striding into the room and actually did step on it! Of course, he didn't fly into the air, but his foot slid forward, he did a split and fell on his side, letting out a horrible yell that left no doubt that he'd been hurt.

Jimmy turned to me, his eyes wide and his mouth agape. I knew it was wrong, but I couldn't help laughing. And I couldn't stop. I fell out of my chair. Jimmy fell down beside me, and we laughed and laughed. I knew we had to stop, knew we were in deep trouble. I was afraid Muscles had really been hurt bad, but I looked at Jimmy, and he was looking right at me, and we started laughing harder. I rolled onto my left side, so I wouldn't see him, to regain my composure, but Gino Ragucci was there on the floor on that side of me laughing so hard that tears were streaming down his cheeks.

Muscles stood up awkwardly, favoring his right leg and holding his shoulder. He glared at us with a rage in his eyes like he might march over and beat us all black and blue. But he didn't. No, what that wonderful old man did, while the lunch ladies scolded us, was sit right down on the floor and laugh himself to tears.

A quote came to mind as I sat alone remembering Muscles and Jimmy and my other childhood friends. "The true source of humor is pathos. There is no laughter in heaven." I went to the bookcase and thumbed through the *Collected Works of Mark Twain* I inherited from my grandfather and searched for the book he wrote it in. I knew it was from his autobiographical writings, not one of the novels, so that sped things up. I'd misremembered it. The original quote from *Following the Equator* reads, "Everything human is pathetic. The secret source of Humor itself is not joy but sorrow. There is no humor in heaven."

That afternoon when Muscles slipped and fell was the last time in my life that I laughed so hard that my eyes watered, and I fell to the ground and grew dizzy and short of breath because I could not stop. I suppose it is an ability most of us lose at a certain age. If I had known, as a child, that I would lose that ability, I would have made it a point to find something funny enough to fall down and laugh myself to tears about every day. But it is too late for that. It is too late for many things.

CINDY'S TONGUE

Cindy's

tongue tasted like cherry bubblegum, but not a fresh piece, like cherry bubble gum still in the mouth, still being chewed, long after the sweetness has gone out of it. But her tongue was in my mouth and that was awesome. It was the wetness and the feeling of it flicking against my own tongue that counted. It could've tasted a lot worse, like cigarettes or whatever, and it still would've been totally cool. Then I thrust my tongue into her mouth and that was even more awesome. She sucked it with her moist lips as I unbuttoned her blouse.

Cindy was a junior and the girlfriend of Louie Balboni, my worst enemy, which made making out with her all the more exciting. I was a sophomore. Louie was a senior, and one of the toughest guys at Seaview High. I wondered where he was and imagined how pissed off he'd be if he knew that I was making out with his girlfriend down in the dark basement of one of the abandoned houses on the condemned block we all called Ghost Town. It was soon to be bulldozed for a new condo development. As if making out with Cindy wasn't awesome enough, she said her friend Diane dug me too and they wanted to go at it with me at the same time. She was coming to meet us, but Cindy said she couldn't wait, so we got started without Diane.

I unsnapped Cindy's bra. She let it slip down her arms and off. She pulled my T-shirt up over my head and tossed it across the dark basement room. We pressed our lips together and fumbled with the zippers of each other's jeans. Cindy kissed up and down the side of my neck. She settled on a spot and gave me a hickey, biting gently and sucking.

"Take off your sneakers," she said. I untied and loosened them and took them off. She took one and tossed it dramatically over her right shoulder into the darkness behind her. She pitched the other over my shoulder. We laughed and kissed some more. She pulled my jeans off and tossed them into the darkness. Footsteps creaked the floorboards overhead.

"Here comes Diane," I whispered.

"Nope." Cindy kissed my ear. "It's Louie."

"What? But how would he know we're here?"

"I told him we'd be here." She laughed.

I crawled away from her and began pawing around on the dark floor for my sneakers, my T-shirt, my jeans. She'd tossed everything in a different direction. The basement door creaked open. My hands shook so violently I could hardly pull my sneaker on. Loud footfalls thumped down the stairs. I got the sneaker on, but it was the left sneaker on the right foot, so I yanked it off. My jeans, where were my jeans? Why the hell was I putting on a sneaker when I didn't have my jeans on yet? Idiot!

The thump of Louie's footsteps came closer. A

small orange glow appeared in the doorway at the bottom of the stairs. In the cigarette's dim light, I saw the outline of Louie Balboni's scowling face.

Cindy giggled in the darkness behind me. "I love to watch boys fight," she whispered.

WHEELIES,

LOVE &

STOP SIGNS

All I wanted in the summer of '75 was for Susie Orlock to like me, really like me. I wanted Susie Orlock to love me. I'd hold my pillow in bed at night and pretend it was her. I wanted to walk around the streets of downtown Rockland Park with my arm around her waist, to buy her pizza at Mario's and play Rolling Stones and Led Zeppelin songs on the jukebox and sit in a booth like the big kids. I wanted to buy a cherry Italian ice and share it with her in the alley between the pizzeria and the Baskin Robbins, wanted both of us to lick it at the same time until we were kissing. I asked Susie if she wanted to be my girlfriend, but she said we were just friends. I hoped I could find a way to change her mind.

Me and my then-best friend, Kenny, used to

ride our bikes to her house on Elm Street and hang around. Kenny liked Susie too, but I thought he just liked her as a friend. He seemed happier hanging out with her and talking like a girl than hanging around with guys, shooting pellet guns and stuff. There was something weird about Kenny like he was from another planet or something. One time I said how cool it would be to do it with Susie and he made this weird face like I shouldn't talk like that. I was beginning to think he was a complete gaywad.

All Susie talked about that summer was Duane. All she talked about was how cool Duane was and how good looking he was. She totally had the hots for Duane, which was stupid, because he was like sixteen going on seventeen and couldn't care less about a thirteen-year-old. She should've been going after guys her own age. Like me.

The night I made the wrong turn in my life and everything started going to hell, me and Kenny were riding our stingrays home from Susie's. Kenny's big thing that summer was popping wheelies and seeing how far he could go on one wheel, which is a sort of lame hobby for a thirteen-year-old that he really should've outgrown already. Like I said, Kenny was kind of weird. He was killer good at it though, I must admit. He could pop a wheelie at the corner of Elm Street and ride on his back wheel up Rutledge Avenue past Maple Street, past Lynwood Street and half way to Oak Street, where we both lived. That was his big lame-ass goal for the summer, to pop a wheelie from Elm Street all the way to Oak Street.

Duane called out to me at the corner of Lynwood. He was sitting there with his arm around his girlfriend. They were smoking. I rode over to see what he wanted. Kenny continued on his one-wheeled quest for Oak Street and beyond.

"Ya wanna to make some money, Thompson?"

"Sure, Duane."

"Cool. I've got a job for ya. Meet me here tomorrow at one."

I liked the idea of making some money, but even more than that I thought maybe if Duane thought I was cool then maybe Susie would think I was cool since she thought he was so cool. Maybe if I was hanging around with Duane she'd say yes if I asked her out again.

The next afternoon I began my career as Duane's assistant and look out. I kept watch while Duane clipped hood ornaments off cars. He knew an old guy with an auto body shop who'd pay him for the ornaments. We'd ride our bikes all over the back streets of Rockland Park and Seaview snagging ornaments off luxury cars, mostly Caddies and Lincolns. There were some Benzes around too, but their ornaments were a little tougher to snag. Lincolns you could snap off with your bare hand. For a Cadillac or a Benz, you'd bend the ornament back and clip the cable with wire cutters. Jaguars were worth the most, but they were rare where we lived and almost impossible to clip because the stems that held them on were really thick. Of course, everyone always talked about how cool it would be to snag an ornament off a Rolls Royce, but that was a car I'd only ever heard about, never actually seen.

We'd work most of the afternoon and go home for dinner. I had to lie a lot about what I'd been doing all day. I guess I got pretty good at it because my parents never caught on. I'd meet back up with Duane after dinner and we'd ride to Lee's Auto Body. Lee didn't ever want us coming around during business hours. I'd wait outside the back door while Duane went in and sold the day's haul. Then he'd come out and pay me my cut.

"What's Lee do with the ornaments," I asked Duane while we were riding bikes over to Mario's for pizza after getting our money one night.

"Duh, he sells them."

"Yeah, but who buys them?"

"Guys whose ornaments get ripped off by little pricks like us, that's who. We provide supply *and* demand, that's what Lee says. He charges them the full price it'd cost to order a new one, sticks on one of the suckers we sell him and keeps the difference. Plus he sells to some of the other body shops who don't have their own black market suppliers."

"Black market suppliers?"

"That's us," Duane said.

I liked working for Duane. Pretty much my whole life had taken place within a couple of miles of Oak Street in Rockland Park. It was cool riding bikes down back streets in other parts of town and even in other towns where I'd rarely ever been. A couple of times we even rode through Lynbrook, Valley Stream and across the border out of Nassau County into Rosedale, Queens.

I felt like I was seeing how the real world worked. That was something my Dad said a lot, 'the real world.' But his 'real world' and the one I was learning about seemed like different places. I was beginning to think my Dad didn't actually know how the 'real world' really worked. It was exciting having to watch out for cops and being prepared to haul ass in case someone tried to catch us.

Duane knew his way around all over the place. He knew all the alleys, trails, empty lots and short cuts. He always laid out an escape plan in case the cops, or a pissed off car owner, showed up. He'd go one way, I'd go another. Cops were basically lazy, Duane said. No cop, except maybe a young, gung-ho rookie, would ever jump out of the car and run after a couple of kids on bikes for something as minor as snatching hood ornaments. The trick was to hit a street with a lot of luxury cars that was near a trail, an alley, a park. If you got quickly onto a route where a bike could go but a car couldn't, you were pretty much home free.

Susie and Kenny were in Mario's when me and Duane walked in. Duane went over to the booth where the big kids were sitting. I went and said hi to Susie. She got all snotty with me.

"Oh, I thought you were too cool to talk to us now," she said.

Kenny ignored me like I wasn't even there. He was staring at Susie and giggling and playing footsie with her under the table, like the little gaywad he was. Susie started laughing and kicking back at him.

"Why don't you just go and smoke with the big kids since you think you're so cool," she said.

She and Kenny started thumb wrestling. They were both giggling like little girls. It was embarrassing. I went over to the booth where the big kids were sitting and bummed a cigarette off Duane. I didn't hang around with Susie and Kenny at all after that, but I still thought about Susie all the time.

The next time I saw them was the day I was hauling ass on my stingray up the dirt trail that ran between the Long Island Rail Road tracks and the Rockland Park Reservoir with a cop running after me. My lungs were burning from riding so hard, so long. Duane had the ornaments, I was clean. If I played dumb I'd probably be in the clear, but I still didn't want to get caught, of course. I heard the whine of an engine behind me, a loud thump, a yell, and a grunt. The cop started cursing his head off. I looked back over my shoulder but didn't slow down

The cop was crumpled on the ground tangled up with a couple of kids who'd come whizzing off a side trail on a homemade mini-bike and collided with him. Their ride, a bike with a lawnmower engine mounted to its frame, was off in the weeds still whining. The back wheel was spinning in the air. I figured that thanks to those two chumps on the mini-bike, I was probably home free but, when I turned back forward, I saw another cop running toward me from the other end of the trail.

I cut right up a side trail that led behind the Rockland Park Recreation Center and toward the reservoir. I rode along one of the dirt trails through the pits, a section of deep holes dug into the dirt where big kids smoked pot and made out. It was easy to fall into one of the holes if you didn't know the trail. I hoped I could lose the second cop there. I didn't stop pedaling full speed, even though every time I looked back it seemed the coast was clear. I finally stopped when I reached the council ring, a circle of logs and crappy old furniture scattered around a bonfire pit. I skid out, hunched over the handlebars, and tried to catch my breath. My lungs and throat hurt so bad it felt like I was breathing fire. My heart was beating like crazy and my thighs were burning from pedaling so hard.

Kenny and Susie were sprawled on a vinyl seat someone had torn out of the back of a car and dragged out there. They were making out. Kenny was on top and his hands were up Susie's shirt. Susie pulled her mouth away from Kenny's and glanced over at me with a snotty look on her puss.

"Get lost," she said.

"Dude, figure it out," Kenny said. "We really don't want you around right now."

He had a shit-eating grin on his face. I wanted to go over and knock his teeth down his throat, but I had to catch my breath and keep riding in case one or both of the cops were still after me. I rode away and left them there.

I was gonna quit after that close call, but Duane gave me a fifty dollar bonus, on top of my regular cut. Plus, he said we'd get out of the hood ornament business for a while until things cooled down. The cops had been coming around to all the body shops, Lee told him. It seems someone nailed the ornament off the Caddie of some big shot who works for the county and when he heard it was happening all over Nassau, he threw a shit fit about it with the County Executive making it out to be this big crime wave. They called all the mayors who leaned on the cops, so the cops had to put on a show of cracking down for a while. That's why they'd been so relentless that afternoon when I almost got caught on the trail.

"Lee knows a guy who'll pay for street signs," Duane said. "We're gonna switch it up and start stealin those for a while."

"What's the guy want street signs for?"

"Who knows, who cares. Lee's gonna pay us for them, that's all I know. From now on we work only at night."

We went to Lee's house one night and he explained the new arrangement to us.

"Here ya go, kid," he said out of the side of his mouth he wasn't holding his cigarette in. He handed a big rectangular vinyl bag to Duane. "It's an artist's bag for carrying paintings and shit.

Congratulations, you're an *artist* now. a *rip off* artist."

He laughed and then coughed and wheezed. He plucked the cigarette out of his lips and pounded his chest with his fist like he thought that'd get his lungs working right again. His eyes watered. He told Duane to carry some art stuff with him and wear jeans with paint on them, so he'd look like someone who ought to be riding around with one of them bags over his shoulder. He showed us where to hop the fence into his yard and the tool shed we were to drop the signs off in. He didn't want us coming around the shop anymore, even after business hours, until he was sure the cops were done stopping by. There was a coffee can in the shed where Lee put the money. Each night we went out, we'd drop the signs and pick up our cash from the night before.

At first, we worked from dusk until 9:30, when I had to be home, but we had a lot of close calls. One night Kenny, Susie, and some other junior high kids rode past on their bikes while we were snagging a Ped Xing sign near the grammar school.

Duane glared at them. "Any of you little twerps rat us out, you're all dead meat," he said.

They were all scared of Duane, so we knew they wouldn't rat on us, but there were close calls with grown-ups too, so we worked out a new plan. My bedroom was on the first floor. It was easy to slip out the window at two a.m. My parents' room was on the second floor and, since they had the air conditioner in their bedroom window turned on almost every summer night, I didn't even have to be all that quiet. I'd meet Duane at the corner and we'd head out.

Duane would kneel down and I'd get on his shoulders with the pliers and vice grips. He'd hoist me up and I'd unbolt the sign. I got quick as a Nascar pit crew mechanic after a few nights out. Zip, zip, zip and the sucker was off. I'd hand it down to Duane and he'd slip it into the big rectangular vinyl artist's bag. I'd jump down off his shoulders, we'd get back onto our bikes and tear ass to the next sign. Stop signs, Yield signs, Slippery When Wet, Railroad Crossing signs; we clipped anything we could get ahold of. We'd work until about four, drop the signs in Lee's shed, and get our cash out of the coffee can.

Things were going really good by August. I was rolling in dough, but I needed to be careful about how I spent it until I came up with a cover story for my folks. I needed some kind of fake job I could tell them I had. We were making even more money off the signs than we'd been making off ornaments. I was riding home up Lynwood Street at about 9:30 at night thinking that, as soon as I had my cover story down, I'd buy a really cool record player I'd seen at Sears and stock up on a bunch of new records. I'd ask Susie if she wanted to come over and listen. She was still going out with Kenny, but I was sure I could lure her away from him. I just had to start hanging around with her again.

Sirens wailed in the distance up ahead. An ambulance tore past up Rutledge Avenue. I turned on Rutledge and headed toward Oak. Two cop cars were parked at the corner their lights spinning and flashing. A woman stood beside her blue Volvo giving a report to one of the cops. She trembled and wiped her eyes. Her voice wavered. A little girl, hugging a stuffed Bugs Bunny, leaned against the woman's thigh. She sucked her thumb. Most of the neighbors were gathered, including my parents.

"He did it," one of the little neighbor kids said to another. "A wheelie all the way from Elm to Oak. He might have made it all the way to Pine if he didn't get hit."

Kenny's bike lay in the street. It was all bent out of shape.

"There he is!" Susie shouted. Her face was red and her cheeks were wet with tears. She pointed at me. She strode up to the cops who were talking with the woman beside the blue Volvo. "That's the boy who's been stealing the signs."

Two of the cops walked toward me.

I looked at my parents standing on the sidewalk among our friends and neighbors.

"Mom... Dad," I said.

They looked at me like I was someone they

didn't know. Because I was.

THUNDER

ZYMBOROWSKI'S

VOLCANO

Long before the legend of Thunder Zymborowski began; before I received the Chuck Bednarik trophy, the Rookie of the Year trophy, the world record, and the Hall of Fame nominations; I was a fat, lonely, giant of a boy named Henry moving from town to town with my crazy but loving mother, Ida. We moved to Seaview, Long Island at the beginning of my freshman year of high school. Arly Reed was the first kid at Seaview High School to talk to me and, although I only knew him for a week, in a strange way I owe all I've become to him.

"You just move to town, Hoss?" he asked when I sat at the desk to his right in Mr. Hardin's second-period study hall.

Desk isn't the word for those things, though. They were those little one-piece jobs with the kidney-shaped, wood grain veneered armrest and writing surface attached to the orange plastic chair designed, apparently, by people who thought only little skinny kids deserved a place to sit. As if a kid like me, six foot five, three hundred sixty pounds, didn't feel out of place enough walking the halls like a dinosaur in chipmunk land, they expected me to fit into one of those. The edge of the writing surface dug into my gut, and my thighs pressed right up against the gummy bottom. I slouched over the goddamn dinky thing like it was some sort of trap that had sprung closed on me.

I really didn't want to talk to anyone, wanted only to sit quietly and read, for probably the hundredth time, *High Window*, my all-time favorite Philip Marlowe mystery, but since the kid went out of his way to talk to me I figured I ought to answer.

"Hoss?"

"You look like that guy on Bonanza," he said.

I couldn't argue. I did look like Hoss from that old show, only fatter. Besides, "Hoss" was a big improvement. A kid at my old school in Jersey had been calling me Baby Huey until I grabbed him by the throat in the cafeteria, held him in the air, and asked that he please never say it again.

Arly was a scrawny dirtbag in a black leather motorcycle jacket, black jeans, black boots and a red bandanna folded into a triangle and worn on his head pirate style. His stringy black hair hung out below the bandanna to his shoulders. A silver skull and crossbones dangled from his left earlobe.

"Where'd you move from?"

"Wildwood, New Jersey."

"Why'd you move to Seaview?"

"My mom heard it was a good place." I shrugged.

"She heard wrong. What part of town you in?"

"Right now we're in the Seaview Motel... until things fall into place."

115

"Seaview Motel, no shit? They found a headless body stuffed under a mattress there one time."

"Cut the crap."

"I kid you not."

"For once Arly's telling the truth," the guy at the desk next to me on the opposite side from Arly said. He was a clean-cut guy in a blue V-neck sweater. "It was in the papers last year."

"Yup." Arly nodded. "She was a hooker, and she was buck naked and headless."

"Maid found her when she was changing the sheets and freaked out," the kid in the blue sweater said.

I was expecting Mr. Hardin to shush us, but it seemed that so long as no one spoke loud enough to distract him from his newspaper, we could talk all we wanted.

"Jimmy Simmons," the kid in the V-neck said. He offered his hand. I shook it.

"Henry Zymborowski," I said.

"You play football?" he asked.

"Not really," I admitted.

"You ought to give it a try. We could use another lineman, let me tell ya." He shook his head and whistled through his teeth. "If you turned some of that...*weight* into muscle, you'd be a killer."

"He don't wanna play no stinkin' football, Simmons," Arly said. "He don't wanna run around in them stupid pads getting all sweaty."

"I suppose you think he'd rather be pulling his pud with you hoods, huh Arly?"

"Simmons!" Mr. Hardin complained. He lowered his newspaper and glared at us.

"Sorry, Mr. Hardin," Simmons said.

"Just keep it clean and relatively quiet, Simmons. That's all I ask."

"Yes, sir."

Arly laughed and shook his head.

"You are such a dick," he said under his breath.

"At least I'm not a criminal," Simmons replied.

"Screw you," Arly mumbled.

Simmons, who could not seem to keep his voice down when he got excited, said, "I'm not the one who's gonna be getting *screwed!*"

"Simmons, for crying out loud!" Mr. Hardin said. "And you stop egging him on, Arlin Reed."

"Yeah, yeah, yeah," Arly grumbled.

Simmons leaned toward me and lowered his voice to a whisper so only Arly and I could hear him.

"One of these days you're gonna go too far and wind up a prison shower whore, and I'm gonna laugh so hard."

"Keep it up, Simmons," Arly whispered back. "You just keep it up, and I'll sick Schmidt on your ass, and you'll be one sorry motherfucker."

"Send him my way any time. Reilly, Cavanaugh and the boys will watch my back in case any of your other dirtbag friends jump in while I'm mopping the floor with Schmidt's face.

And I'll bring my little sister along to whoop you."

Every time we moved to a new town, my mother would say, "don't worry honey, you'll make some friends." She never said, "you'll have good teachers," or "there'll be a good library in town," or anything like that. The way she talked you'd think making friends was the most important thing. It was that, and the fact that I hated sitting in the motel room watching her pace, chain smoke, and circle classifieds while talking a mile a minute about how everything was going to work out sooner or later, that made me say yes when Arly asked if I wanted to hang out after school. I was happy to have something to do on a Friday afternoon and could tell my mother I'd made some friends.

We stopped beside a house with a chain link fence around its yard a few blocks from the school and checked that the coast was clear. Arly, Schmidt, and Rodriguez hopped the fence, darted across the side yard, and hunkered down beside a large bush. I walked around front and went through the gate. When I came lumbering up behind them, Schmidt was pushing on the frame of a small basement window. He was solidly built and strong, not quite six foot tall, with long blond hair and pale gray eyes. He looked angry even when he smiled. The window swung up and in. Schmidt held it up while Arly squirmed through and dropped to the floor. Rodriguez handed the twelve pack Schmidt bought with his fake ID down to Arly then squeezed through. Rodriguez was shorter and thinner than Schmidt but wiry and strong.

"Go, Hoss," Schmidt said.

"I can't fit through there."

"Sure you can. Blow out and suck your gut in."

"Look at me, man." I held my arms out to my sides. "There's just no way."

"Quit stallin, ya big pussy. Do it."

I got down on hands and knees and backed up to the small window. I put my left leg in, then my right and pushed back until my hips and ass barely squeezed through. My legs were hanging down inside against the wall. I felt Rodriguez and Arly grab my ankles. My hands were pressed to the dirt outside in push up position. My arms began to tremble.

"I'm stuck! Pull me out."

"Get ready," Schmidt said. He set one of his black motorcycle boots on my shoulder. "Suck that gut in, fat boy."

He stomped my shoulder and my arms gave out. Arly and Rodriguez yanked my ankles. My gut, chest, then chin scraped the splintery old weather-beaten windowsill. My T-shirt caught on a big splinter, got pulled up under my arms and tore. When my chin hit the windowsill, I bit my tongue. I dropped through the window, landed on my feet in the basement, and fell onto my back.

Arly and Rodriguez jumped me and started punching my stomach and laughing.

"Blubber, blubber, blubber!" Arly shouted.

Rodriguez said, "Fat, fat, fatty! Big fat Hoss."

And that's when it happened, that's when I got the first little glimpse of my future as the

121

legendary Thunder, that's when I first felt the full force of what I've come to think of as my volcano. It was like a switch inside my head, that I didn't know how to control yet, got switched to ON and suddenly an enormous source of energy was at my disposal. It surged through my body. I sprang to my feet much faster than I'd ever imagined I could move, grabbed Arly around the waist and flung him onto my shoulder. I latched my free hand around Rodriguez' throat and slammed him repeatedly against the far wall opposite the window.

Schmidt, who'd climbed through the window after I dropped in, punched me between the shoulder blades and that sort of snapped me out of it. I stood there panting and tasting the iron-rich flavor of the blood from my bitten tongue fill my mouth. I pressed my tongue against the roof of my mouth.

"Big Hoss," Schmidt said. "You're all right, man." He slapped my shoulder.

We both noticed that Rodriguez's tongue was sticking out. He was gagging and his eyes were bulging. Both his hands were clamped around my wrist. I released my grip and Rodriguez slumped to the floor. I put Arly down. We all stood there looking down at Rodriguez as he regained his breath. My heart was pounding like crazy and I was trembling all over. It was like I'd been forced through that little window into becoming some new kind of person.

"Wow, man. I'm really sorry. Guess I just freaked for a second."

"Strong motherfucker," Rodriguez rasped. He shook his head. I reached out, took his hand and pulled him to his feet.

The room we were in was empty except for a workbench along one wall with a pegboard above it. The shapes of tools; hammer, pliers, a row of crescent wrenches in size order, etc. were drawn neatly in black marker around the spot where each tool once hung. I was suddenly reminded of my favorite toy at the pre-school my mom used to leave me at while she was waitressing. That was from the first time we lived on Long Island, years before, when she was with the second or third man she was with after the guy who was my father.

She asked, on the drive down Garden State Parkway from Jersey, if I remembered anything from those old days. I didn't at the time but there in the basement, I remembered that toy, that little red wooden toy workbench with holes of various shapes; stars, squares, diamonds, and circles cut out of its top. I never tired of fitting the bright blue, red, orange, green circles, squares, stars into their appropriate holes.

Schmidt led the way into the next room. We sat on the crappy old pea green shag carpet. Arly opened the twelve pack and handed us each a can of beer. Rodriguez pulled a ziplock bag full of black pills from his pocket and tossed it onto the carpet. He glanced at me.

"You like speed?"

"Never tried it."

He shook four pills out onto his palm and washed them down with beer.

"It'd burn some of that fat off," he said.

124

Arly took two of the pills from the bag and Schmidt took two.

"Try a couple," Arly said. "Black Beauties, man. They're killer."

I took two pills from the bag and washed them down with beer. Rodriguez took out two more and handed them to me.

"You should take more," he said.

I popped them into my mouth and washed them down. Schmidt pulled a hard pack of cigarettes from an inside pocket of his denim vest. The vest was originally a jacket but the sleeves had been cut off. The cover art from a Black Sabbath album was painted on back. He flipped the top of the cigarette pack open, looked in and moved the cigarettes around with his pointer finger. He tipped the pack, held the cigarettes in place and shook out a joint. He lit the joint, took a hit, and passed it to Arly.

"Is that paint thinner still here?" Rodriguez asked.

Schmidt exhaled. "In the boiler room," he said.

Rodriguez stood, walked to the boiler room and opened the door. Arly passed me the joint. I took a hit. Rodriguez came back with the can of paint thinner and a white rag. He sat down, doused the rag with paint thinner, held it to his nose and inhaled deeply. The smell of the paint thinner filled the room and mingled with the pot smoke. Rodriguez leaned back against the wall and giggled. I passed him the joint. Arly took a turn with the paint thinner then gave it to Schmidt. When Schmidt finished with it, he passed it to me. I doused the rag, held it to my nose as they had, and inhaled. We passed the joint until it was spent and kept on with the paint thinner for a while longer. Arly passed out another round of beers and then another and another. Schmidt lit a second joint and passed it. I was flying.

Rodriguez started to laugh, then Arly did.

"What's so funny, man?" Schmidt asked.

"Fuck, man," Rodriguez said. "Damn."

Arly laughed and slapped the floor. He lay down with the back of his head cradled in his hands. "You see Fiona Steinway in them jeans today? Sweet! The seam was crawling right up her ass crack, man."

"That bitch is fine," Rodriguez said.

"Hell, yeah, she is," Schmidt said. "I'd like to just throw her down and bone her, man." He leaned back on his elbows, raised his hips, and humped the air. "Bam, bam, bam! Just bang her silly, man."

"I'm lit, man," Rodriguez said. "I'm toast."

"We need candy," Arly said.

Schmidt punched him on the shoulder.

"You hear that," Rodriguez asked.

"I didn't hear nothin," Arly said.

"Shut up," Rodriguez said. He held up his hand. "Listen."

We got quiet. The floorboards creaked overhead.

"The real estate lady," Schmidt whispered.

He stood and stalked silently back to the

window we came in through. Arly, Rodriguez and I followed. Schmidt boosted Arly up and out. Rodriguez pulled himself up and scrambled through. He held the window up while Schmidt climbed out. Schmidt looked down at me standing there alone in the basement.

"Guess you better hide, man," he said. He lowered the window and ran off across the lawn.

I hurried back, as quiet as I could, past the empty beer cans, paint thinner and rag to the boiler room. I heard the door at the top of the basement stairs open. There were voices. A light came on. I opened the boiler room door, stepped inside and pushed it closed behind me. I stood where the door would open in front of me. It was a lightweight hollow frame door. I could hear them talking pretty clearly once they came into the room.

"It smells sort of funny down here," one of the women said.

"Well, I'll admit it is a little musty," the other woman, the realtor, said.

"Haven't smelled *must* like that since my college days," the man said. "Looks like we just missed a party."

"I don't know what to say," the realtor said. "It's really such a lovely neighborhood. I promise you, I'll be calling the police as soon as I get back to the office. We'll make sure nothing like this happens again."

"Just some kids screwing around, I guess," the man said.

The boiler room door swung open and the light came on. I was sure they could all hear my breathing behind the door, could hear the rib-rattling pounding of my stoned, speed-crazed heart.

"Wow, the boiler's seen better days," the man said. "We'd have to replace that."

"Let's have another look at the kitchen, honey," the wife suggested.

"Yes," the realtor agreed. "Let me show you the kitchen again."

The man flicked the light off and pulled the

129

door shut. I stood in the darkness trembling and listened to them clomp back up the stairs. I waited for the sound of a door slamming or a car pulling away. I waited until I could wait no longer and, although I had no idea if they'd gone or not, I stepped out and hurried up the stairway to a side door off the basement landing. I opened the door and hurried away as fast as I could.

Arly, Rodriguez and Schmidt were watching for me from the far corner.

"Damn, boy, we thought you must've strangled them," Arly said as I approached.

"Fat Hoss, the Jersey Strangler," Rodriguez said.

Schmidt slapped my back. "Can't hang out there no more," he said.

"Let's go over to the grammar school field and smoke another joint," Arly suggested.

"Yeah, that whole scene fucked up my buzz," Rodriguez said.

We smoked the joint behind the backstop of the softball field in a corner where the tall chain link

130

fence was overgrown with vines. When we were done, we wandered across the field to the school building. Three kids were playing stickball against the wall outside the gym. Two of them looked about our age but the third, who was playing outfield, was a little junior high kid. He looked exactly like the kid at bat, only smaller, so I figured they were brothers.

We sat on the cement stoop that led up to the gym doors and watched them play. I hadn't smoked pot in months and had never smoked so much at once before, plus the speed, beer, and paint thinner. Sitting there on the stoop, I started to buzz all over. It began in my fingertips and nose and spread throughout my entire body. My head got wobbly and loose feeling. I imagined it bobbing like the head of one of those little spring necked Chihuahuas people had in the rear windows of their cars. My stomach felt like it was full of writhing, oily worms. The back of my throat was tight and the spit in my mouth was hot.

"Is my skin humming?" I asked.

"No, it's Friday," Arly said.

"When?" Rodriguez asked.

"Today," Arly said.

"I know today, but when?"

"What?" Arly asked.

"I want candy *now*," Rodriguez said.

I decided if I concentrated on watching the game maybe I'd forget the fact that enormous moist snakes were wrestling in my stomach and that my arms were whistling hymns I remembered from those old Sundays at church during my Mom's brief religious phase. The pitcher wore a faded purple T-shirt with cut off sleeves that said *Saints* across the chest. Beneath that was a logo that read Catholic Youth Organization Basketball League. On the back, the name Gallagher was emblazoned across his shoulder blades over the number 10.

"Never seen you guys at the high school," Schmidt said. "You go to Saint what's-her-name's?"

"Yeah," the pitcher answered.

132

"Hey, no batter, no batter, no batter!" the little kid out in the field taunted his brother. The pitcher wound up and threw the faded day-glo green tennis ball toward the strike zone, a gray rectangle painted on the brick wall. The batter swung the bat, which was just a little thicker than a broomstick, and swatted the ball way out over his brother's head.

"Chase that, weasel dick!" he shouted. "No batter, my ass."

"Hey man, Rodriguez said. "You Catholic school fairies really take bubble baths together?"

"Fuck you," the pitcher said.

"My friend's just joking with you, man," Schmidt said. He laughed. "Hey, how about a game?"

"There's four of you," the batter said.

"I'm just gonna watch," I volunteered.

The batter looked at the pitcher.

"I don't have to be home for an hour," the pitcher said.

"Neither do we," the batter said. He turned to Schmidt. "Okay."

Schmidt stood and walked over toward the batter who gripped the bottom of the bat and held it upright in front of him. Schmidt wrapped a hand around the bat above the kid's hand. They went hand over hand that way until the batter's hand was flush with the top. Schmidt crowned it with his hand.

"First up," he called.

He took the bat, stood at the wall beside the strike zone and took a few practice swings. The kid who'd been at bat stood behind the crack in the blacktop that signified the pitcher's mound. His friend stood where the blacktop ended and the softball field grass began. The little kid moved farther back on the grass to play outfield.

"Hey no batter, no batter!" he shouted. He punched his bare hand like a baseball player punches his mitt while he waits for the pitch. The pitcher wound up and threw the tennis ball. Schmidt swung with all his strength and missed.

"Whiff!" the outfielder shouted.

"Come on, Schmidt," Arly said. "Nail the sucker!"

Schmidt swung hard at and missed the next two pitches also. Instead of handing the skinny bat to Rodriguez, who was up next, he cocked it over his shoulder and skipped across the blacktop toward the pitcher chanting, "la-la, la-la-la, la-la, la-la-la."

"What the hell?" the pitcher said. He began to backpedal.

Schmidt ran at him, planted his feet, and swung the stickball bat as hard as he could slamming it right across the boy's mouth. The boy fell to the ground. He shrieked and covered his face.

"Home run!" Schmidt shouted. He held his arms over his head, the bat in one hand. He leapt up and down laughing, threw the bat aside and started kicking the crying boy on the ground.

The outfielder shouted, "Billy!" and came running to help his big brother.

The other kid was stunned. He stood there with

his hands beside his face and his mouth open. Rodriguez and Arly jumped up from the stoop beside me and charged across the blacktop howling. Rodriguez kicked the stunned kid in the stomach and the head, then pummeled him with a flurry of punches. Arly ran for the little kid who raised his fists like a boxer. Arly tackled him, pinned his arms to the ground with his knees and punched him repeatedly.

And as for me, what did I do? I wish I could tell you that I rose to the occasion, that I was brave like my fictional hero, Philip Marlowe, private eye, that I fought against Arly, Rodriguez, and Schmidt to help those kids, but what I did was puke on my sneakers. When I finished with that, I ran away.

"Jesus Christ, Arly," I said when I passed him. "Jesus."

He didn't look up. I lumbered across the field and out the gate we came in through to look for a phone to call the cops. An old man was walking a Collie up the street. I headed toward him but stopped, put my hands on my knees and ralphed again. The old man and the Collie came to me. The man placed his hand on my shoulder.

"You all right, son?"

I stood. The old man took his hand away and looked up at my face.

"Call the cops, Mister. Some kids are getting beat up on the schoolyard really bad."

"Come on, let's get you cleaned up," the old man said.

"I'll be okay, just call the cops. Please."

The Collie looked at the man and barked twice. She and the old man trotted down the street, up a brick stoop and into their house.

I got to study hall early the following Monday and asked Mr. Hardin if I could change my seat. He looked at me funny but said sure and assigned me the desk beside the door in the front row. I opened my book, *The Simple Art of Murder*, lowered my head and read. I was going to ignore Arly when he came in. He was no friend of mine. It would be better to have no friends than to have friends like that. I'd spend my after-school time at

137

the public library reading detective novels as I had in so many towns before. I was used to being a loner.

Arly never showed up for class that day. In fact, he never came back to school at all. Neither did Schmidt or Rodriguez. I overheard one of their dirtbag friends in the cafeteria say the cops knew exactly who to look for when the Catholic school boys described their attackers. Arly, Schmidt, and Rodriguez were in juvenile detention. Juvie the dirtbag called it. They got out of juvie eventually but didn't come back to Seaview High. They were sent to some kind of special school for bad kids instead.

It's funny how sometimes the stupidest thing can change your whole life. Getting stuck in that goddamn basement window turned out to be the best thing that ever happened to me. I'd always dreamt of losing weight, getting in shape and all that, but I was never motivated enough to stick with it until I became obsessed with the memory of being stuck in the window and that crazy adrenaline rush I got after those guys forced me through. I told myself I'd never let anything like that ever happen to me again, that I'd never be the sort to get stuck in a window or to run away when innocent people needed help. I became determined to find a way to tap that crazy energy that rushed through my system that day in the basement.

I read every book on exercise and healthy eating they had at the library. I started going to a nearby rec center to lift weights, swim, ride the stationary bike and sweat in the sauna. Whenever I didn't feel up to it, whenever I was ready to quit, I'd remember my big tubby ass stuck in that window. I'd think about the volcanic sensation I had, the incredible strength I found that day. I'd use the memory to push myself to lift one more set on the weights, swim one more lap, stay on the bike ten minutes longer than I did the day before.

Things started going pretty good for me in other ways too. My mom got a waitressing gig at the Seaview Diner and hooked up with this divorced guy named Alfonse who ate there a lot. He wasn't too bad a guy. He sold used cars for a living and customized classic Chevies for a hobby. Alfonse was a recovering drinker and drug addict and he went to those twelve step meetings all the time. He got my Ma started going too, although she was only addicted to cigarettes and coffee, not booze or hard drugs. He said she was what they called an enabler which was why she always hooked up with drunks or druggies. It was on account of her taking care of her drunken parents while she was growing up, he said. She couldn't help but go looking for more of the same. Anyhow, he helped her figure out some stuff about herself. She was happy when they were together. They were good for each other.

Alfonse even paid for me to go see this doc about my eating disorder. I hadn't ever heard of that before, an "eating disorder." I'd always just figured I was born to be a fat kid. Alfonse taught us both to meditate too. I owe a whole lot to Alfonse. We moved into his house, eventually, and I had my own room.

Week by week the fat wore off and the muscle went on. I got stronger and stronger and

140

discovered that I could actually eat *more* when I worked out regularly, that so long as I ate the good healthy food I needed, it was okay to throw some junk food on top, as long as I worked it off. I decided I would try out for the football team sophomore year, like that kid Jimmy Simmons had suggested. I spent the summer working out even harder and reading everything I could find about football and exercise.

One Friday night in August, I was sitting alone in Burger King chowing down and reading *They Call Me Assassin,* the biography of the legendary Oakland Raiders linebacker Jack Tatum, when I heard someone say, "Hey, Hoss." I looked up and saw Jimmy Simmons waiting in line at the counter. He was holding hands with Fiona Steinway, who I'd been thinking about an awful lot. She looked amazing in her designer jeans, pink tube top, and feather earrings. They walked over and Simmons shook my hand. Both he and Fiona had hickeys.

"Hi," Fiona said.

"Hi," I said.

141

It was hard to look at her without, you know, *looking* at her.

"Damn, look at you Hoss," Simmons said. "You're a lean, mean fighting machine."

"Yeah, well I've been working out like crazy."

"Coach Barker tells me you're trying out for the team."

"Yup."

"Excellent. Hey, did you hear the news about our boy, Arly?"

"No, what?"

"Him and his loser friends got busted for killing a guy."

"Cut the crap."

"I kid you not. You know that retarded, old fag who made change at the arcade?"

"Jimmy!" Fiona scolded.

She slapped his arm.

"What?"

"That's no way to talk, Jimmy Simmons. That

poor man is dead."

Jimmy looked up at the ceiling and moved his lips silently like there was something he just had to say but knew he better not let her hear. I guess Fiona was right about it's not nice to talk that way, but I must admit I knew at once which one of the change guys at the arcade Jimmy meant from that description, knew at once he meant the strange little man with the wispy gray hair and thick glasses.

"He was out having his smoke break behind the building next door to the arcade," Jimmy continued. "They dropped a cinder block on his head from the roof."

"That's sick."

"Tell me about it. That psycho Schmidt finished him off with a fence post. They were trying to break into one of the stores through a skylight on the roof but couldn't get it to break. Extra thick plexiglass or something. When they saw the old guy down there, they decided it'd be a whole lot easier to rob him instead. Killed him dead for a bag of quarters and a roll of singles."

"Those guys are animals."

"No, you, *you're* the animal, Hoss. Look at you! You look like the goddamn Hulk! Don't he look like the Incredible Hulk, Fiona?"

"Well, except for not being green and all, yeah."

"You're going to be a superstar on the gridiron, Hoss."

"Thanks. I hope so. We'll see how I do."

"No, I'm serious, man. You'll do great, take my word for it. I've got a sense for these things."

Simmons was right. I was good from the start because of my exceptional size and, as the years went by, I got better than anyone imagined possible. All of the rage and sorrow, loneliness and confusion, all of the fear from the uncertainty of my early life, the constant moving from town to town, my mother's procession of loser boyfriends, the constant worry we'd end up sleeping in the car again or worse, all that drove me to eat and eat and eat to pack on the weight as if it might insulate me from my troubles, I channeled into working out and playing football.

I told myself over and over that everything wrong with my life would become all right if I'd crash through the line and trash the quarterback, that girls like Fiona Steinway would want to be around me if I'd crash through the line and trash the quarterback, that' I'd be rich and my mother and I would never have to worry about money again if I'd crash through the line and trash the quarterback. I meditated, visualizing myself as King Kong and the opposing line as thin balsa wood figures.

I learned to control the volcanic sensation, envisioned a switch inside my head that set it off at the sound of a ref's whistle. I chugged blenders full of protein powder, fruit juice, eggs, bee pollen, and brewers yeast concoctions and lifted weights until the veins bulged from my enormous arms, shoulders, neck until I could feel the skin stretching from my expanding muscles. By senior year it was ridiculous for me to be playing on a high school team. Opposing offensive lines triple-teamed me. The college scouts were circling.

I won the Chuck Bednarik Trophy for best defensive player in college and defensive rookie of the year my first year in the pros. I was a regular pick for the All-Star Team as I continued my march toward the record books and the Hall of Fame. My friend and teammate, Lonny "Speedway" Jones, the great running back, gave me my nickname, but it was a sports writer for The New York *Daily News* who gave him the idea. He wrote, "Zymborowski lunges off the line like lightning, crashes like thunder..." The next day "Speedway" slapped my shoulder and said, "there he is, Thunder. Thunder Zymborowski."

It stuck. The night I planted Dale Montgomery in the astroturf, breaking Reggie White's record of 176.5 career sacks, the fans in the stands whod painted their faces blue with a gold lightning bolt down the middle stood and stomped and clapped and chanted louder than ever.

Stomp, stomp. Clap, clap. "Thunder! Thunder!" Stomp, stomp. Clap, clap. "Thunder! Thunder!"

During the post-game interview, I thanked God, my Mom, my stepdad Alfonse, my wife, my teammates, and all my coaches right back to Coach Barker at Seaview High. It didn't occur to me until later that I should have thanked Arly, Schmidt, and Rodriguez for forcing me through that basement window into my new life.

POTATOES IN
BROOKLYN

There

was this guy I knew when I was in my teens, who everyone called Potatoes. I don't know why they called him that. It was a nickname he'd acquired before I met him. He was a fat, stupid slob with bad breath and body odor who made up idiotic knock-knock jokes.

We stole a car together, a beater of a blue Chevy Caprice Classic. It wasn't something we planned. We'd spent the day drinking a case of Schmidt's at a secluded corner of Silver Lake Park in Baldwin, the town on Long Island where we both grew up. We were sitting under the big tree everyone called "the big tree" which was a meeting point for kids in the neighborhood. It was a hot August afternoon. We were out of beer and out of money, so we got up and left.

"Well, what the hell are we gonna do now," I asked as we wandered up the hill out of the park. "I don't have to go to work for another two hours."

"You're too drunk to work."

"I can pump gas drunk. Hell, it's easy." I stepped on a loose, round stone hidden beneath the tangled grass. It rolled beneath my shoe, and my ankle twisted. I fell.

"Yeah sure," Potatoes said.

He let out a short laugh, then grabbed my elbow and shoulder and helped me up. He began to speak, but something caught his eye. I followed his gaze. There she was, parked at an angle far from the curb, abandoned, apparently, by someone in a hurry who'd left the windows down and the key in the ignition. We looked at each other and laughed.

Don't ask me why I let Potatoes drive. Guy's got a nickname like that, I should have known better. He turned the key, stepped on the gas and threw her into gear. We screeched away from the curb into the blare of the horn of an oncoming delivery van. The Playboy bunny air freshener swung wildly from side to side beneath the rearview mirror.

"Guess I'll buckle up," I said.

"Good pickup on this bad boy."

"Uh... *yoh.*" Sometimes a simple yeah or yup aren't enough and you've got to go for the uh... *yoh* for emphasis.

Potatoes slowed down and took us on a tour all through Baldwin and Freeport. I pawed through the glove compartment and then shoved my fingers into the gap between the torn white vinyl seat and backrest hoping to find money for beer. The ashtray was full of old butts that were smoked down to the filters. The radio antenna was a bent wire coat hanger.

Neither of us said so but I knew he was hoping, as I was, that somebody'd see us and ask where we got the car. I wanted to be admired for my

153

spontaneity and bravado, to be thought of as someone reckless and criminally heroic. Of course, we didn't see anyone we knew.

Did I tell you that this took place in 1982 on the day following one of the best parties I'd ever attended, that I'd been making out in the darkened basement with Margaret Doherty, a freckled, black-haired girl I'd been crazy about since fifth grade who was behaving foolishly because she was drunk and had recently been dumped by her boyfriend, a girl far too beautiful, intelligent and popular to be involved in any way with someone like me, that I had her jeans unbuttoned and was pulling them down when she stood and pulled them back up so she could go pee, that I waited alone in the dark, watching the glowing red numbers of a digital clock change from 2:02 a.m. until 2:19 a.m., for her to return then slunk upstairs and found her making out on the couch with my ex-friend Conner, that I'd begun drinking with a vengeance after that, stayed in the kitchen past sunrise with a couple of other die-hards and set a new personal record for alcohol consumption before puking and passing out in the backyard, that I'd had only about two hours of sleep on the dewy lawn of that home I expected never to be invited to again and was still drunk when I stood and staggered to the Dunkin Donuts, chose one Boston Creme and one Boysenberry jelly, got slapped on the back by Potatoes who said, "Hey John, long time no see," and decided to go drinking with him? Have I told you that this was the summer I graduated from high school?

Potatoes would have graduated three or four years earlier, I think, but never did. He just stopped going, as I heard it. He was cousins with my friend Tony from auto shop, which is how I got mixed up with him. They weren't real cousins, though, just "mothers-are-best-friends" cousins. Tony, who was, as far as I knew, Potatoes' only tenuous link to anything resembling a social life, hated him. He always made fun of him behind his back. We all did.

Potatoes lived in his mother's basement where, when he wasn't washing dishes at Sonny's Ristorante, he seemed to spend most of his time smoking cigarettes and watching TV, the same thing his mother did on the first floor and her lodger, Mr. Sloane, did on the second. It was a depressing place to visit. We only went there as a last resort when we'd failed at every other attempt to acquire beer or booze and needed Potatoes to buy us some. Or on winter nights when there weren't any house parties and it was too cold to drink outside.

Potatoes drove past the pool hall on Grand Avenue, behind which Scotty Rizotti and his whole gang of little hoodlum friends got the shit kicked out of them by three black kids from Freeport back in seventh grade, continued on past the public library and pulled a tire-squealing right turn onto Sunrise Highway nearly nailing a shiny, new, black Beamer that was parked near the corner.

"Always wanted to see Montauk Point Lighthouse," he said.

"It's nice."

"Been there?"

"When I was a kid."

As we entered Merrick, it dawned on me that Potatoes was driving far worse than could be attributed to mere drunkenness.

"You've never driven before, have you?"

"Once."

He turned his big sweaty face at me and smiled. There was still some orangey muck on his teeth along the gum line from the barbecue potato chips we'd been eating in the park. His right front tooth was a dead one, brown, crooked and chipped.

"Anytime you want me to drive, just say the word," I said. "I've got a license and everything."

Potatoes darted his head left and right to calculate time and distance as we approached the next intersection. Without bothering to slow down or get into the left lane, he pulled a screeching, nearly-up-on-two wheels U-turn around the divider and started heading back west. A chorus of horns from every direction accused us of stupidity.

"Good idea. I've got to get to work soon

anyway."

"Nope," Potatoes said with a determination in his voice that was unfamiliar to me.

"Nope what?"

"Nope we ain't going back."

"What are you saying?"

"I'm saying we're never going back to that goddamn town again!" His voice was quavering.

"Potatoes --"

"We're going to Colorado."

"On what? We're both flat-on-our-ass broke, remember?"

He looked down at the fuel gauge.

"Plenty of gas."

"Three quarters of a tank is *not* going to get us to Colorado!"

"We'll worry about getting more when we run out. I want to see my cousin. I ain't seen my cousin since we were both eleven. She's got to be all grown up now, Cassie." He turned to me and grinned. "That was the other time I drove, when Cassie and her family came to visit. We had a big reunion and everyone was happy, mostly. That was before my father went to Texas and never came back, before everything turned to shit. I went with my uncle and my dad to buy beer and watermelon and stuff, and on the way back we pulled into that shopping center in Oceanside. You know the one that's sort of across from the dump but not exactly?"

"Yeah."

"It was closed because it was Sunday afternoon. My dad let me sit on his lap and steer around in the empty lot. Remember that, when stores were closed on Sundays?"

"Yeah, or open only half the day. Everyone put on a necktie and went to church. When did all that stuff change?"

"Nineteen-seventy-three," Potatoes informed me. He continued his story. "We came back to the house and I told everyone how I drove. Cassie asked my uncle could she go there and drive in

159

the lot, too, and he said 'no' and she said 'why' and he said 'because you're a girl.' She cried and stomped her feet in the kitchen and sulked all afternoon. I felt so bad for her, having to be a girl and all."

"Well," I said, "have a nice trip. Just drop me at the Chevron on your way to the interstate."

Potatoes glared at me with an intensity that made his fat face appear almost chiseled and lean. "You're starting to piss me off, John," he shouted. He ground his teeth and his jaw muscles twitched. Then his mood turned suddenly joyous. He bounced up and down on the seat chanting, "we're gonna go see Cassie, we're gonna go see Cassie!"

The car swerved hard into the center lane cutting off a jacked-up primer-gray Dodge Dart with big mag tires which veered into the right lane cutting off a black Ford Bronco. Another flourish of horns announced our re-entry into Freeport. The gray Dart came up beside us in the left lane and the driver, a muscular, tattooed guy in his late twenties wearing mirrored sunglasses, shouted a long, impressive chain of expletives at Potatoes rounding it up with, "pull over, shithead! I'm gonna give ya a drivin lesson you'll never forget!" He shook his fist.

Potatoes first sneered at the guy like he thought he might try to intimidate him but, seeing that was unlikely, his expression softened and he began apologizing profusely and making excuses. I gazed across the highway at my boss, Craig, and co-worker, Jerry, talking beside the gas pumps as we roared past the Chevron. Fortunately, the guy in the Dart was satisfied with humiliating Potatoes and didn't feel he needed to drive us off the road and kick the crap out of the both of us, a feat I was sure he could've accomplished without so much as getting winded. He turned left at the next corner and drove on into the rest of his life, a life I sincerely hoped would never again involve me in any way.

We continued west through Freeport and Baldwin into Oceanside. How foolish I'd been for wanting to be seen in this stolen heap with Potatoes. I hunched down in the seat, turned on the radio, adjusted the dial from the oldies down to the classic rock station and sang along with Robert Plant while I strategized a means of wresting control of the car.

"Now just what the goddamn hell is that supposed to mean," Potatoes inquired as I sang along about a cloth, a hand that sews time, a feather, the wind and so forth. He was trying to sound cool, but I could tell he was still shaken.

"Aw, it's just stoner talk," I said.

"Hey," he explained, "I've smoked plenty of damn weed in my day, but I never thought of anything like that to say!"

"Well, I guess that's why Robert Plant's in Led Zeppelin and you're not."

He laughed, shook his head, and sailed through a red light at the intersection of Long Beach Road. A horror-stricken young woman in a brand new white Honda punched the horn and skidded and swerved to keep from hitting us. Potatoes flipped her the bird while arching his neck back over the headrest and trying to match Plant's high-pitched keening as Jimmy Page began his guitar solo.

"Aw, aw, awwwwaaaaaauuuuugh!" Potatoes caterwauled, Stevie Wondering his head from side to side.

I closed my eyes and did the unimaginable. I prayed for a policeman, prayed to be pulled over and arrested for grand theft auto, anything to put an end to this. Kids who were far stupider than I but who behaved themselves, studied, did their homework, had never gone to school drunk or stoned, who'd never been suspended, were preparing to head off to college in a few weeks while I, local drunkard, gas jockey, ne'er-do-well, one of the ones the teachers and counselors shook their heads and frowned about, a potentially promising but somehow doomed, damned, or in certain immeasurable but important ways dumb, student was being chauffeured toward my death by a sweaty alcoholic with no driver's license and little reason to live.

"Let's see what this baby can do," Potatoes said. He stomped the gas and roared through Rockville Centre and Lynbrook managing somehow to squeak under every light as it was turning yellow. Where, for Christ's sake, were all the goddamn cops? We didn't hit a red light until Valley Stream. For some reason, Potatoes decided to stop for it.

"All right, you've had your fun. My turn to drive."

"Dream on," he replied.

"That's it," I said. "I'm leaving." I opened the door and began to step out, but the light turned green and Potatoes stomped the gas pedal. We raced off. The door swung shut slamming my shin, pinning my leg against the doorframe, and twisting my already sore and swollen ankle as my sneakered foot dragged bumpily along the asphalt. I pushed the door open and pulled my leg back in.

"Son of a fuckin bitch you goddamn stupid motherfuckin idiot," I shouted.

Potatoes remained silent and kept his gaze straight ahead. He was grinding his teeth again. I was shaking as I pulled the leg of my jeans up to my knee to look at the wound, a bloody scrape that would soon, no doubt, be surrounded by a dark bruise. I eased the denim back down over my shin and sat up. My head felt wobbly like my neck had turned to sponge. The world was breaking into tiny pieces before my eyes, and my lips were tingling as if being rapidly poked by a million pins.

I was going to make my move as soon as we stopped at the next red light, slam the sucker into park and pummel Potatoes, throw him out of the car and drive myself home. I folded my arms over my chest, sat back in the seat with my eyes closed and took a few deep breaths to prepare myself.

"Wake up," Potatoes said, shaking me, as I emerged from a dream about running and fighting, a dream swirling with snarling dogs, into the gray-yellow smelling smog of his breath.

The world had grown dark. The streetlights were on.

"How long did I sleep?" My mouth was so dry that my lips hurt at the corners when I parted them to speak.

Potatoes did not answer. "Let's have some pizza," he said.

I stepped out of the car onto the sidewalk of a street that I'd never seen before. My ankle was stiff, swollen and numb. My shin was throbbing. The denim of my jeans was pasted to it with dried blood. The skin around the wound felt hot and tight. I was groggy, disoriented and had a pounding headache. Everything I looked at, the few thin trees growing near the curb, the cars, the people walking past, appeared slightly foreign.

Potatoes walked in a happy, bouncy way that annoyed me. "You like Queens?" he asked. "Man, I love Queens! You must've been really tired, John.

I've been driving around and around all over the place. Getting pretty damn good at it, too! There's the college that my cousin goes to." He pointed across the street where, behind a tall chain-link fence, there was a ballfield lit up by bright lights atop high steel poles. A game was in progress.

"I thought your cousin lived in Colorado." I said.

"I'm only allowed to have one cousin? You didn't drink any water last night did you, John? You need to drink more water when you drink alcohol so you don't get dehydrated. One glass of water to every three glasses of beer, that's what I do. I'm thinking maybe I should get my GED and then go to college. Have you ever thought about going to college?"

"Yeah. Recently I've been thinking it doesn't seem like such a bad idea. Kinda wished I'd thought about it sooner."

I limped after him past a corner gas station to the pizzeria, slowly remembering how angry I was at him. The pizzeria was air-conditioned, and it smelled fantastic, as though we'd stepped into the corner of heaven devoted to the worship of garlic. An Italian tenor sang opera from a speaker behind the counter. Although that's not the kind of thing I usually listened to, it sounded mighty pretty just then, and I was happy to be in the cool air knowing that I'd be eating soon and having something to drink.

Potatoes pulled out a wad of cash.

"Hey, wait a minute. I thought you said you were broke?"

"I lied."

"What the fuck?"

"We didn't need any more beer, John. Sometimes you don't know when enough's enough."

He turned his attention to the man behind the counter. The man had thick, dark hair on his forearms and greenish tattoos half-covered by the short sleeves of his white T-shirt. He removed a pie from the wide steel oven with one of those huge wooden spatulas and sliced it into evenly sized wedges. Potatoes addressed him in Italian.

"You want the whole thing, pisano?" the guy responded to whatever it was Potatoes said.

"Yup. This is a special day, and my friend and I are very hungry."

Aside from a few potato chips, I hadn't eaten

anything since the donuts.

"I didn't know you spoke Italian," I said.

"I've been picking it up at work," Potatoes replied. "Plus I got some tapes and a book from the library."

"Wow. You're not Italian though, right?"

"Nope."

"Polish?"

"Lithuanian."

Potatoes jerked his head to the left and wiggled his eyebrows up and down. I looked. There were two girls, young women really, older than me, sitting at a corner table drinking through straws. The drinks were in big glasses, the type you'd be served an ice cream sundae in, and topped with whipped cream.

What's to say about these two women? A couple of tubbies. I'd have never looked at them twice. A brunette and a redhead. The brunette had a great big ass that bulged over the side of her seat. Probably really nice people, the sort it would be okay to live next door to and argue jokingly with about the Mets versus the Yankees and stuff like that once in a while, but nothing to raise your eyebrows and make a big deal about. I looked back at Potatoes and shrugged.

He paid for the pie and two large Cokes. We carried it all over to a little table near the women.

"Knock-knock," Potatoes said as soon as we were seated. He looked past me, over my shoulder, at them.

"Who's there?" I heard the two of them answer, as if it was nothing out of the ordinary to have some goofball come up to you like that.

"Can't you see it's me? There ain't no door between us," Potatoes said.

I looked down at my plate and shook my head, but the women laughed like they thought it was the funniest thing they'd ever heard. I couldn't believe it. They seemed to have a case of whatever the hell it was Potatoes had. So then the three of them were yakking away and it was decided we should put our tables together and all share the pizza. They couldn't believe I'd never had an Italian soda before, so they ordered me a hazelnut flavored one. It tasted really sweet and was ice cold. I was glad to have it in addition to the Coke.

The women told us they were both grammar school teachers taking night classes to get their masters degrees. They were celebrating tonight because they had just finished their last test of the summer semester.

"Do you guys know Angela Komentauskis," Potatoes asked. "She's my cousin."

The women looked at each other then both shook their heads and said, "no."

"I think she's studying history," Potatoes added.

"It's a big school," the redhead said. She put her hand across the table to me. "By the way, I'm Connie," she said.

I shook Connie's hand then the hand of the brunette, who introduced herself as Barbara. Their hands were cool, from holding the icy glasses, and

171

soft.

"I'm John," I said. I looked at Potatoes, whose real name I did not know. Even his mother had called him Potatoes the times I'd heard her yell down to him from the top of the basement stairs. It seemed all of a sudden, important that his name was a mystery, and I was excited to find it out.

"Everybody calls me Potatoes." He shrugged and laughed.

"What an adorable nickname," Connie, the redhead, said.

"And it totally fits," Barbara said.

"Doesn't it?" Connie agreed.

Somehow they got into this big conversation about the Kosciuszko Bridge, of all things, and it turned out Potatoes considered himself an expert on the subject, having read two library books about the bridges of New York recently. I slid another cheesy slice from the tray to my plate and sprinkled garlic powder onto it.

"Oh, the Kosciuszko is totally underrated," he said shaking his head. He furrowed his brow and folded his arms across his chest. "I mean the Brooklyn Bridge is the Brooklyn Bridge, don't get me wrong, a league of its own. But the Kosciuszko, she's a sweet little bridge." He nodded and gazed out the big plate glass window at the cars buzzing by on Kissena Boulevard. "Yeah, a sweet bridge in her own right."

I couldn't even imagine having an opinion about something like a bridge. I ate my pizza in dumbfounded silence merely nodding and "um-humming" from time to time. I figured Potatoes was simply bullshitting them about the library books, trying to pass himself off as a smart guy to these teachers, but then he started spouting facts.

"It opened in 1939, if I'm not mistaken, and was originally called the Meeker Avenue Bridge before being renamed in the forties in honor of the great Polish patriot Tadeusz Kosciuszko, who fought in the American Revolution."

"That's right," Connie said. "But the old Poles in my neighborhood pronounce it Kosh-key-you-shkoo."

"Kosh-key-you-shkoo," Potatoes repeated slowly as if it was terribly important to pronounce it just the way the old Poles in Connie's neighborhood did. He'd been saying "Koz-key-you-sko."

Connie turned and exchanged a look with her friend.

"He has *got* to talk to Vince," Barbara said.

"That's just what I was thinking," Connie agreed. "Vince loves the Kosciuszko. It's his favorite bridge."

"*You* are coming to CoCo's with us," Barbara said, gazing into Potatoes' eyes in what I thought she intended to be a sexy way.

"You *are*," Connie re-emphasized. "And you too, of course," she said turning to me and patting my forearm. "Any friend of Potatoes is all right with us."

So we got back into the Caprice and followed the ladies in Connie's crappy maroon Trans Am. Potatoes concentrated on driving well, now that he had someone to impress. He managed to keep

174

us in one lane, for the most part. I got the feeling that we were taking a long, roundabout way of getting where we were going and realized why when I saw the bridge up ahead. We'd gone out of our way to take a ride over the Kosciuszko. The bridge seemed poorly designed to me, too steep and narrow, but I guess there was something sort of charming about it.

Eventually, we parked on Flatbush Avenue and walked a couple of blocks. CoCo's was a long narrow room with a bar on the right and a row of booths along the wall on the left. No one bothered to card us at the door. I was disappointed since I'd recently bought a drivers license from this twenty-three-year-old guy who looked sort of like me and I wanted to try it out.

The air was hazy with cigarette smoke. Frankie Valli and the Four Seasons sang "Rag Doll" from the jukebox. A group of guys who couldn't have been much older than me sat at the first booth closest to the entrance and a row of old men hunkered on stools along the bar. Three women seated in the next booth talked and laughed really loud. The one facing me was dressed in a postal carrier's blue shirt and shorts like she'd come straight from work. She laughed so hard at whatever it was that her friend had said that she took off her glasses and wiped tears from her eyes. Two couples in their forties were throwing darts in the back.

Connie and Barbara led us to the booth of young guys, introduced us and told them how we'd met at the pizzeria in Flushing. I think one of them was Connie's younger brother. He had red hair and kind of looked like her. Plus she spoke to him in a different tone than to the others, like she had some say in how he conducted himself.

At the far end of the bar, a big blond-haired man in his early thirties stood up from his stool and shambled toward us. He was around six foot five and had a big beer gut. His forearms were thick and veiny like he tore phone books in half for a living, but I got the impression by the slow way he walked and his smile that he was one of those easygoing guys who got along with everyone and was hard to piss off. He put his arm around Connie's shoulder, hunched down and kissed her.

"Vince, this is Potatoes and his friend, John."

We both shook hands with Vince. He ordered a pitcher of beer while the rest of us squeezed into the empty booth. He carried five glasses with his fingers thrust into their mouths and held the pitcher just below his chin like it was a mug he planned to drink himself. He sat and poured the beer. We all tapped glasses.

While the rest of them got onto the topic of bridges, the Kosciuszko in particular, I sang along under my breath with Ricki Lee Jones about Chuck E. being in love, glad that the oldies on the jukebox weren't all really, really old. Vince told an anecdote about someone jumping off a bridge and Barbara said something about a boat ramming into a pylon of one.

The man Vince had been sitting beside at the bar before he came and joined his girlfriend Connie and the rest of us turned around on his stool. He was an old guy wearing black-framed glasses and a dark blue baseball cap with no insignia above the bill as if it had escaped the factory before being branded. He had a red face and a gin-blossomed nose.

"The Kosciuszko? My grandfather built the Kosciuszko," he announced. His look turned serious. "Not by himself, but, ya know, he was one of the guys." He smiled and nodded before turning back to his drink and cigarette.

"Old Karl," Vince said. He shook his head.

I stood and hobbled back past the dart players toward where I figured the men's room must be. It had one of those long, old-fashioned trough urinals that three or four guys could pee in at the same time, which is pretty weird if you think about it. Since no one else was there, I stood at the near end and pissed an arc down to the far end just for the hell of it. The door creaked open and Vince stepped in. I quickly turned and peed straight ahead feeling like a silly kid. He passed behind me, unzipped and pissed at the far end.

"Potatoes seems like a good guy," he said.

"Oh, yeah," I answered. "One of the greats."

"I'm sure glad Barb met him. She's really been down on herself since her last boyfriend dumped her. Guy was a jerk. Never liked him."

"A real prick, hunh?"

"Yup. Some guys just never know how good they've got it. A girl like Barb, totally devoted to doing right by a guy...." he shook his head. "Potatoes, though, he seems all right."

I thought it was funny that Vince was talking about Potatoes and Barbara like they were already an item, but when we walked back out I saw that the two of them were lip-locked and swapping spit.

Vince said he wanted to buy me a shot and asked what I'd like. I said I'd like an Alabama Slammer, a drink I'd heard of but never actually drank. It was sweet and smooth at first but then burned at the back of my throat. Connie slipped out of the booth, came over and wrapped her arm around Vince's waist. She looked up at him and they shared a smile. Then she looked at me and

179

winked. Vince ordered another pitcher for the three of us. Connie sat on Vince's old stool and we stood beside her.

They asked questions about how long I'd known Potatoes and stuff. Although they were only making conversation to pass the time while the new lovers got acquainted, it made me uncomfortable. I felt like I was being tested.

Potatoes whistled. He had a certain way he did it through the side of his mouth that I'd never seen anyone else do. It made a distinct sound. I turned and looked. He tossed the keys, and I caught them. I dropped them into my pocket and ambled over to the booth.

"What's up?"

"I'm going to stay with Barb tonight. There's a party in Williamsburg. It's going to be an older crowd."

"Yeah, yeah. I get the picture." I stuffed my hands into my pockets and glanced toward the door. "I better be getting back anyway." I didn't like being given the brush off. The fact that

Potatoes was older than me felt different than it had before. He seemed to be talking down to me.

"You're all right, John." He held his hand up for a high five. I slapped it. "You're one of the better people I've known."

I limped out of CoCo's into the Brooklyn night and wandered up Flatbush Avenue looking for my stolen car. The world seemed a far bigger place than it had that morning. I liked the way that enormity felt around me.

After a brief panic about getting lost on the unfamiliar streets and running out of gas in a strange neighborhood, I found the parkway and knew I'd get close, if not all the way home. I drove the speed limit and stayed in the right lane. I felt fine but knew it had to be an illusion. I'd drank myself sober, as they say, another personal first.

I thought about Potatoes as I drove, about how we'd used him and insulted him behind his back. I understood now that he knew it all along. I tried to imagine what sort of person I looked like through his eyes. It didn't make me feel good about myself.

I figured the last place the cops would look for a stolen car was the place it disappeared from, so I pulled up to the very spot where we'd found the Caprice and got out leaving the windows down and the key in the ignition. Everything was just as we found it except that I parked straighter and closer to the curb, and the gas gauge was on E. I limped downhill into the park toward the big tree. I wanted to find Tony and everyone and tell them about our big trip to Queens and Brooklyn.

I heard laughter and shouting in the distance to my right and saw a cigarette lighter flash. A cluster of shadowy figures wandered through the darkness in my direction. I heard a bottle smash on the asphalt path and recognized Tony's too loud laugh. Ducky Simms shouted his lame Steve Martin impersonation, "Well excuuuuuse me!" There was more laughter and incoherent shouting, and I could see the six or seven of them staggering along, pushing and antagonizing one another.

I held my right hand up beside my mouth to shout out to them. Then I changed my mind. I lowered my hand. I turned and walked back up the hill alone.

DAMN WEED

The summer I graduated from high school, my grandpa busted me smoking pot behind his garage. I was just hanging around, looking forward to getting the hell out of my hometown and starting college. I'd stop by Grams and Gramps place about once a week to check in on them and help with the chores.

When I first got to his place that afternoon and started mowing the lawn, Gramps came striding out the backdoor and across the grass pretending to be mad at me. He was a square-jawed, square-shouldered old guy who walked like Gary Cooper on the way to a gunfight, but his scowl was pure Clint Eastwood. His shirt was loose, his pants baggy, due to the muscular atrophy of age. He never bought new clothes.

"Where the heck am I going that I gotta look snazzy," was his usual reply whenever my Mom suggested he go buy himself some new duds.

"Dang it, I got nothing to do all day *but* mow the damn lawn Roger," he said as if appalled at my lack of consideration for coming over and doing some of his work for him. He smiled and clapped my shoulder. "Good to see you, boy. Well, all righty. Go ahead and help if you're set on it, but save me some."

Gramps never got a power mower, which was probably one reason he was still strong and healthy at eighty-two while his friends were all shuffling around with walkers, drooling on themselves in nursing homes, or dead. He got his exercise. It'd sometimes take him as long as a week to mow his front and back lawns. He'd leave the old wooden handled manual push mower wherever it was when he'd gotten too tuckered out to continue. Next morning he'd push it some more until the heat got too much. Little by little he'd get it done, take a few days off, and start over again. The trick for me was to help some, but not too much. He really didn't have much else to do.

After Gramps went back inside, I decided to take a quick smoke break. I stepped behind the garage, took my pipe and stash out, and smoked up. I'd gotten this weed from my usual dealer, who mostly peddled shitty Long Island ditch weed, but he was like, "no dude, this is the real deal, man. Mexican weed, bro. Real sweet bud."

It did smell seriously strong and sweet but I gave him the 'yeah, yeah, yeah' treatment, not expecting much based on the usual crap I got from him. Holy God almighty though! Wow! I smoked up one little bit of bud and was soon gigglingly, prophetically, religiously high. Crazy high! I was King Kong size and walking on clouds. I looked around at the shrubbery, hedges, grass, the leaves of plants, the leaves of trees. People, have you any idea of the number of shades of green? Can you understand the beauty of dusty white paint peeling off gray clapboards on the back of an old man's garage? Ants were tunneling in the earth below the grass plotting our overthrow, but it was okay. We humans have had our time here. Let the ants have it, I said to myself. Let them fucking have it.

Gramps was striding toward me again when I stepped out from behind the garage. He wasn't scowling his fake scowl though, it was his real scowl. His eyebrows were equally lowered, denoting actual anger, rather than the one brow cocked up, one low, fake mad scowl. I whistled a few bars of the "Good, the Bad and the Ugly," theme song and giggled.

"Something's burning, Roger, and it don't smell like tobacco," Gramps said.

If I'd been smoking the usual ditch weed I'd have gotten all neurotic and paranoid in such a situation but, on the magical, mystical Mexican wonder weed, the world was beautiful and all was well.

"Had a feeling you were mixed up with that stuff," Gramps continued. Your Grams said to me she said, 'do you think Roger's on drugs?' And I said, 'Emmy, it wouldn't surprise me.' You've gotta knock it off, Roger. That damn weed'll rot your brain, make you crazy, suicidal. You've got a good head on your shoulders. I'd hate to see you throw it all away on account of that damn weed."

"Ah hell, Gramps, all you know about weed is that crap you read in the papers and see on TV. That ain't nothing but a mess of propaganda laid out by the corporate screwheads to keep working people like us in line. All they care is that we wake by seven, get to the job by eight, and do all their goddamn work for them. They're scared that if people smoke up and sit back they'll see the big picture, catch on to the scam, and shut down the machine."

Gramps tensed his jaw and squinted. All this pot smoking commie crap I was talking was pissing him off most seriously. If he'd have been forty years younger and I was a stranger, not kin, he'd have probably whooped my ass. Gramps was quite the street-fighting badass back in the day, according to family legend. I kept at it though.

"Look Gramps," I said, "how can you knock pot when you've never even tried it?"

He nodded. He didn't have any quick comeback for that argument. Gramps was a sucker for that kind of logic. He'd fought in World War II and got angry anytime he heard that someone who hadn't been there was writing a book about it. If they weren't really there, they couldn't really know what it was like, he always said. That was the first chink in his wall of defense. I kept talking. What exactly I said, I can't recall, but it worked. I was soon behind the garage again smoking a bowl with my eighty-two-year-old grandfather.

What in Christ's name was I thinking? I guess I hoped Gramps would try it, not go crazy, not get suicidal, that his brain would not rot, and that he'd stop worrying about me. I guess I hoped he'd accept it, accept me as a pothead. I guess it never occurred to me that he might like it. Really, really, really like it.

*   *   *

I was kicking back in my room, running the usual fantasy about my ex-girlfriend through my mind, giving my right arm a serious workout. The phone rang. I dried my hand, pulled up my jeans and picked up the receiver.

"Hello?"

"Is your mom there, Roger?"

"No Gramps, she's out."

"Good, good, Roger. That's good. Listen, I told your Grams about the smoke... you know, about behind the garage."

"Yeah?"

"Yeah. She wants in."

"She wants what?"

"She wants to give it a whirl, you know? You only live once, she says."

"Grams wants to get high?"

"That's right, Roger. Hook us up, buddy."

I knew if Mom ever found out I'd be dead meat, but I did it. I bought my grandparents a

193

dime bag, a pipe, and screens, some rolling papers. I smoked up with them, gave Gramps the lowdown on ditch weed vs. good weed, how to clean the pipe screen, how to roll a decent joint, all of it. We sat cross-legged on the living room floor and passed the pipe.

"Hee-hee! Oh boy! Damn."

"What's so funny, Gramps?"

"Durned if I know. You hungry?"

"Yeah."

"Hows about you go make us three ice cream sundaes, Emmy?"

"No, I think it's Tuesday. Isn't it Tuesday, Roger?"

Grams scratched the scalp beneath her gray curls. Her horn rims were crooked. I took hold of the arm of her glasses that'd somehow gotten loose and placed it back behind the appropriate ear.

"It's Thursday, Grams," I said.

"I don't care what dang day it is," Gramps said.

"All I'm saying is I'd like some ice cream."

"I knew it was one of the 'T' ones," Grams said.

"Hey, I've got an idea," Gramps said. "Whatever day it is, hows about you go make us three ice cream sundaes, Emmy. And I'll start a fire."

"It's June, Gramps."

"So?"

"Well... um, just kind of a weird month to get the fireplace going."

"We can stare at the flames."

I must have been stoned as shit, because somehow that made sense to me, building a fire in the fireplace so we could stare at the flames on an eighty-five degree June day.

"Say, hows about I go make us some ice cream sundaes," Grams suggested.

"Good idea, Em," Gramps said. "I'll have hot caramel."

"Hot fudge for me, Grams. Thanks."

She had trouble straightening her old legs out and getting up off the floor. I stood, took one of her hands in each of mine, and gave a gentle tug.

"Upsy!" She giggled like a child and tottered wobbly toward the kitchen.

"Never try to sell a man something he doesn't want, Roger," Gramps said.

I followed him out the back door into the yard.

"Okay, Gramps."

"That's one thing I learned in the insurance racket. Damn crabgrass." He crouched and yanked the weed from the lawn. He stood, shook dirt from the roots, and stuffed the weed into his shirt pocket. "Learned that early on. Some fellas never figure it out. Cribbes who I worked with, have I ever told you about Cribbes, Roger?"

"Yeah, Gramps."

I'd heard plenty about Cribbes. He was Grandpa's great example of how not to be. I imagined the man dressed like a raggedy little Charlie Chaplin tramp with a sad clown mask permanently painted on his face.

196

"Cribbes never learned." Gramps grimaced and shook his head. He took his key ring from his pants pocket and unlocked the padlock on the side door to the garage. He turned and glared at me. "Cribbes *never* learned," he reemphasized. He flipped the hasp and opened the door. I followed him through the doorway into the dark garage. He tugged the string dangling from the overhead pull chain and the light came on.

"He'd spend an hour on the phone, Cribbes would, then tell you 'I almost had 'em, *almost* had 'em!' 'Almost,' I'd say. 'What the hell good is *almost*, Cribbes? You gonna feed the family *almost*? Give the wife a handful of almost to take to the butcher shop?' 'I like the challenge,' he'd say. 'Okay, Cribbes,' I'd tell him, 'you take the challenge and I'll take the money.'" Gramps shook his head and let out a laugh. "Cribbes," he said. "Goddamn Cribbes!" He turned to me. "You can hear it in their voice, Roger! Soon as they pick up the phone, you can hear it! Once you've trained your ear, of course."

I held my arms out, palms up. Gramps grabbed

logs from the pile and started loading me up.

"'Hello?' the son of a bitch says. Right there and then, Roger! Right, damn, there and then you can tell whether you're speaking to a man who wants to buy insurance or not. I wish I could tell you how, Roger, I really do, but it's something you've got to learn on your own. You've got to train your own ear."

"Okay, Gramps. Okay." I had no intention of ever going into insurance sales but knew if I'd said so I'd have had to put up with a speech on why I should.

Gramps stopped rambling once we got back inside and got the fire going. Who knows how long we stared at the flames. Five minutes? Five thousand years? Something like that. I'd become completely transfixed by the world of fire -- red, orange, yellow, even a little green and white heat leaping from the logs, wow!

"I think your Grams must've forgot what she was about," Gramps said.

"Huh?"

"Shoulda been back in here with the ice cream by now."

"Oh, yeah." I'd forgotten about the whole sundae thing. "I'll go check."

Grams' head was back over the chair. She was snoring. The upper plate of her dentures was pillowed, teeth up, on the pea green fabric of the house dress between her thin, veiny thighs. The separate stripes of strawberry, vanilla and chocolate ice cream had melted into a brownish pink puddle of soup which was leaking from the corners of the thin cardboard box across the pine tabletop. Hot fudge and caramel bubbled and boiled over their respective pots on the stovetop.

*　　*　　*

The next time I stopped by, the front door was wide open but no one seemed to be home.

"Gramps? Grams?" I called out in the living room. "Hey, guys? Hello," I shouted in the dining room. I walked into the kitchen. "Anybody home?" The back door was open. I walked out into the yard. Grams and Gramps were sprawled on the lawn flying a pale green kite.

"Look what your Gramps made, Roger," Grams said as I approached.

"Had all I needed right in the shop," Gramps said. "I was puttering around, you know, and there it was, a green kite just asking to be made. Heavy green paper, dowels, rag for the tail and fishing line. All this wind today; funny to have such a windy day in July. I swear I ain't built a kite since you were just a little bitty fella, Roger. You remember that?"

"Kind of, yeah. We went to the beach."

"That's right. It was the same week as the eclipse."

"Yeah, you also made that cardboard peek hole look-at-the-reflection-in-the-water thing that week, so we could all see the eclipse without going blind."

"That's right."

"And you read me that part from that book..."

"*A Connecticut Yankee in King Arthur's Court...*"

"Wherein he reads the almanac and then pretends to cause the sun to go out by timing it for when he knows an eclipse happened."

"You got a good memory, Roger."

"Roger, I was just telling your Gramps about this gal, Daisy, I knew when I was a girl in Pennsylvania," Grams said. "This Daisy, she was a wild one. Not bad, just wild. Some folks, they can't see the difference, though, you know? So she had a reputation, Daisy."

"Yeah?"

"Well, she liked to take off her dress and swim naked in the river summers. Let me tell you, that's not the sort of thing a decent girl did in them days, Roger. Oh no, not in Pennsylvania mine country, no sir. I'd cluck my tongue and nod with all the other girls and women when they'd say how bad she was and how, just you wait and see, one of these days she's gonna get what's coming to her. But in the back of my mind, I was sayin to myself, I was sayin, well why not? What's so wrong with it, and whose business is it anyway? I told myself one day I was gonna go down there to the river and swim in the buff myself, but I never done it. I never done it, Roger. I never had the guts."

Grams started to blubber. She'd always been a stern, tough sort of woman, but had turned sentimental and blubbery in her late seventies. It seemed to set in at the same time as her senility. She remembered in great detail the events of a day sixty years ago but couldn't tell you what happened five minutes ago that very morning. Gramps reached over, with the hand that wasn't holding the kite string, and squeezed Gram's shoulder.

"There, there, Em. We ain't dead yet. We'll go do us some skinny dipping before the summer's out, I promise."

"Oh boy... I'm, uh... I'm gonna go get something to drink ... or, uh... something..." I stood and wandered quickly away across the lawn feeling a tad queasy.

* * *

"Quit Bogarting the bowl, Roger."

"All right, all right, Gramps, chill out. I didn't get a decent hit the first time."

I passed the pipe. Gramps took a long hit and held the smoke in his lungs a minute, eyes closed, savoring the sweet bud. Smoke began drifting from his nostrils. He exhaled out his mouth.

"You know who smoked pot, Roger? Thomas Goddamn Jefferson, that's who! Ben Franklin? Pot farmer! I've been reading up on it, Roger. It's a Goddamn outrage. The founders of this great nation of ours smoked pot, but can we? Oh no, some damn putz came along and made a law!"

"Preaching to the choir, Gramps."

He seemed to have forgotten that I was the one who'd turned him on to weed. All of a sudden he was the big expert. Gramps had always been obsessive. Whenever he got into something new, he really got into it.

"God made pot, Roger. Man made booze. Who do you trust?"

"Uh, yeah, Gramps. Heard that one before."

* * *

The curtains were all drawn. Jazz music, bebop, was playing inside. This was very strange. Grams and Gramps were Lawrence Welk people, Mitch Miller people. I rapped the knocker twice, used my key, and walked inside. The living room reeked of pot. Grams was seated on the floor cross-legged. Gramps was beside her reclined on one elbow. A black man, not quite so old as the two of them, but no kid, was sitting cross-legged across from Grams. A giant glass hookah with six tubes sat on the floor between them. The hi-fi was also on the floor, surrounded by scattered LPs and their cardboard sleeves. The four big speakers were arranged around them in a sort of mini Stonehenge arrangement.

It was nice to see Grams chatting happily with a black guy. She'd been a bit of a racist and a bigot most of her life, quite frankly, but that was one of the things she'd forgotten about when the senility set in. The only black folks I'd ever seen in their house were the blind piano tuner and his mother, who drove him on his rounds. They came by once a year to tune Gramps' little, second hand, upright Steinway.

"Well, hello there, Roger," Gramps said as I approached. "You ever meet Louis, the young fella who tunes our piano?" Gramps asked.

I nodded.

"This here's his dad, Louis Sr. We struck up a conversation at the record store and it turns out I've known his wife and boy for years but never met him. Ain't that something? You ever think about stuff like that, how you know someone from work or wherever for years and years but their whole life can remain a mystery? I was thinking about this one fella I used to work with. Have I ever told you about Cribbes, Roger?"

205

"Yeah, Gramps. I think you might've mentioned the dude once or twice."

"Cribbes was always talking about his wife, what he and his wife did over the weekend, where they were going for vacation, etc. He had her picture on the desk, lovely gal. Too lovely to be running around with a putz like Cribbes, that's what I thought. I never met the lady in person and she never once called the office. Not once! What kind of a wife never calls the office?"

"Maybe she was a deaf mute," Louis Sr. Suggested.

"Oh, he'd have mentioned something like that," Gramps protested. "Nope, she never called because she never *existed*. It didn't occur to me until just now but I'm sure of it. It was all an act. Ol' Cribbes was a sissy. Lived down in Greenwich Village for Christ's sake. Didn't ride the train out to the island or up to Westchester like a regular fella. And he was always going to the theater, him and his imaginary wife. Now a real man, he goes to the theater maybe once a year because it's his wife's birthday and she wants to go to a goddamn play, of all things, so he holds his nose and goes. Ol' Cribbes, he was a sissy all right. Why the hell didn't I catch on 'til now?"

"What's it matter?" Louis asked.

Gramps glared at Louis but his face softened and he smiled. "Ah hell, you're right, Louis. What's it matter? Why it doesn't matter at all." Gramps turned to me. "Guess what, Roger? I've got a new dealer thanks to Louis here. Just in time with you heading off to college soon. All you gotta do is tell the cat behind the counter at the record store that you're looking for an Al Green record and wink. They got the goods right there in the back. How about that?"

"Hmmph." I smiled and shook my head as if this was news to me.

"You like Coltrane, Roger," Gramps asked. "Louis here turned me on to this bebop music. Never liked the stuff before, but I just didn't get it. Let's face it, Roger, I was a square. I've been a square all my damn life. How'd it take me eighty-two years to get hip?"

*   *   *

A Miles Davis song was playing when I rode up the driveway on my bike, "Deception" from *The Birth of Cool*. It was coming from the back. Gramps had set the speakers in the windows of the sun porch so he and Grams could listen while they worked in the garden. They both had their big floppy straw hats on. Gramps had his shirt off. He was wearing a pair of pinstriped suit pants that had been cut into shorts above the knee, and sandals.

It shouldn't have been such a big surprise, I guess -- Grams and Gramps had always been excellent gardeners -- but I totally freaked out when I saw the tiny stalks with those familiar leaves.

"Gramps, this stuff is illegal! You can't just grow it out in the yard next to the tomatoes. Someone might see them and rat you out to the cops."

"I know it, Roger. Don't think I don't know it. That's why we're moving the whole operation down the basement. Know anything about hydroponics, Roger? I ordered a kit from this outfit I found in the back of *High Times*. I think I got a handle on it, but I could sure use some help."

Luckily I was off to college in a week, the perfect excuse for backing out on helping Gramps with his new venture.

* * *

My roommate had gone home for the weekend so I took advantage of the added privacy. I was kicking back in my dorm room, running the usual fantasy about my ex-girlfriend through my mind, giving my right arm a serious workout – but wait, no, that's misleading. It wasn the *old* same old routine about my old ex-girlfriend, it was the new old routine about my most recent ex-girlfriend -- when the phone rang. I dried my hand and pulled up my jeans.

"Hello?"

"Roger... oh Jesus, Roger. I don't know what to say..."

"Mom, what is it? What's wrong?"

"You're grandparents...."

"Are they okay?"

"I don't know. I mean yes, they're fine, they're not in the hospital or anything, but..."

"But what, Mom?"

"I think they're..."

"What?"

"It's crazy but... oh forget it, Roger. Never mind."

Gramps called right after my Mom hung up. He was talking like a complete wild man, really out there. I was worried one of his new connections had turned him on to mescaline or acid, but Gramps reassured me.

"Mescaline? Acid? You think I'm a maniac,

Roger? I'm just about the weed, man; I'm all about the weed."

*   *   *

Christmas was weird. Gramps was high as a buzzard circling over a dead wildebeest waiting for the lions to get their fill and go, an analogy which occurred to me because I'd witnessed that very scenario the night before on a PBS documentary. Grams kept falling asleep. Ma was darting these glances at me like I was supposed to know why they were both acting so weird. I kept launching these wide-eyed *what the heck do I know, I'm just a kid* looks back. Then my dad called drunk from this bar in Denver, where he'd moved with his fiancee, sobbing about how she'd dumped him and asking us all what was so bad about him that everyone always dumped him. It was a relief to be done with vacation and get back up to school.

*   *   *

I had an out-of-state internship that summer, so was only home to visit for a week. The basement farm was quite impressive, but it would take a lot longer than Gramps realized to grow weed potent enough that anyone would want to buy it. He was way out ahead of himself.

"Distribution, Roger. It's all about distribution. You can be producing the sweetest damn bud on earth, but what good is it doing you if you're not getting it out to the consumer? An excellent, high quality-product at a fair price, that's what we're aiming for here. It takes time to produce quality bud, Roger. I know it, but in the meantime, I'm getting the other pieces in place. We're gonna start local then expand our reach, build infrastructure then branch out up and down the coast. That's long range. I'll tell you, Roger, it feels damn good to be back in the business world. I've got a reason to wake up in the morning again. Retirement? It's a crock, Roger, a crock. Never retire. A man needs to stay active."

*   *   *

When I returned for Christmas break, I was relieved to find Gramps had given up on the homegrown idea. But it turned out he'd gotten into something far heavier.

"Hell, Roger, who were we kidding? Me and Louis finally realized we could never produce anything to compare with what the big boys down in the islands are growing. We're in tight with these Jamaican cats now. Yes sirree, I'm done with the farming. From now on I'm all about transport and distribution. Look at me, Rog! You're old Gramps is the perfect mule! White as a ghost! Pale as paste! Old as the hills! I'm back and forth a couple times a month. Breeze right through customs like a harmless old fart. The pigs never suspect me. Hell, I can even fool their dogs!

*   *   *

A couple of months later, though, Gramps met his match, a Narc with a drug-sniffing dog even he couldn't fool. Grams got put in a home. It made me feel mighty sad and guilty visiting Gramps in the pen. He looked surprisingly fit. He leaned forward nearly pressing his lips against the mouthpiece of the thick safety glass between us.

"Listen, Roger, get off the damn weed, you hear? It'll rot your brain, make you crazy, self-destructive. Look what it's done to me!"

I wanted to remind Gramps that I'd been smoking weed a good deal longer than he had and that my brain hadn't gone to rot. In fact, I had a 3.85 average and had made the dean's list.

"I'm doing okay here, though. I really am," Gramps said. "I've made some good friends. You get an idea about people in prison from the media but I'll tell you what, there's some good fellas in here with me. Most of these guys are innocent. You'd be amazed, Roger, how many innocent guys get framed by the man."

"Yeah, Gramps? That so?"

"You're damn straight it is. For the black cats, especially. A poor black man without a lawyer? Forget about it. The cops pounce. They got quotas, you understand? They gotta write a certain number of tickets, lock up a certain number of people, and they don't give a rat's ass if they guys they lock up are guilty or not, some of these dirty cops. That's a fact, Roger. My eyes have been opened. But I'll tell you what you ought to do, Roger. Get off the damn weed and go get yourself some weights. Your ol' Gramps is all about pumping the iron these days, Roger. Not a goddamn thing else to do in here other than get out in the yard with the fellas and lift. Get yourself a good solid bench for doing your chest workout, Roger, and a curling bar for the biceps so you don't put a strain on your wrists. And get yourself a set of dumbbells for your chest flies and your shoulder flies and your bent over rows and so forth. You gotta have a set of dumbbells, don't let anyone tell you otherwise. And nutrition, damn it! You gotta eat right, Roger. Your workouts aren't worth a damn without the right fuel."

215

Gramps drew back the short sleeves of his orange jumpsuit and flexed his biceps. He had a serious set of guns on him for an old dude.

"Look at that Roger, eh? An eighty-four-year-old man! Now you get started with the weights today and imagine how strong and fit you'll be by the time you're my age. But don't forget your stretching and cardio, Roger. Big biceps won't do you a bit of good if your heart and lungs ain't worth a lick, for Chrissake! It's about strength, flexibility, and endurance, see? You want the whole package. Don't be one of those stupid lumps who's all upper body but walking around on a set of chicken legs. You gotta work the legs, too, Roger! Don't leave out the legs!"

"Okay, Gramps. Okay." I didn't have the least bit of interest in bodybuilding but somehow I couldn't tell him that.

"What good is all that muscle up top if you've got no foundation under it? See what I'm saying, Roger? Squats, Goddamnit! Do your squats, Roger! Leg curls, leg extensions, and calf raises, they're all vital. Get yourself a subscription to

216

Muscle and Fitness and read it religiously. That's what it takes, knowledge and dedication!"

It pains my heart to say this, but it was an enormous relief when the guard came back and led Gramps away. He was tiring. It was all my fault that he'd gotten locked up, and yet he never ratted me out to my Mom. I'd gotten good at telling myself that prison was good for him to try and ease my guilt. He was in tremendous shape and staying out of trouble, but it bothered me that he'd die in prison. Or so I thought until my mom called. She was frantic. Some Feds and local cops had been by the house. It seems there was a jailbreak.

SCOOTER

Saturday

morning I was lying on the couch in my undershorts waiting for my girlfriend to call when someone knocked at the door. I opened the door but didn't see anyone. Then I looked down. A leathery-faced guy with no legs was staring up at me from a wide skateboard device he was perched on. He had three jagged, yellow teeth in his gums; two up top, one on bottom. One of his eyes was a popeye and the other a lazy, droop-lidded one. He was wearing a short-sleeved, denim pullover with a pair of large pockets, like the sort for holding nails on a carpenter's apron. He cleared his throat, licked his chapped lips, and began to speak.

"Maybe you can help me, pal," he asked.

"Maybe," I answered. "What seems to be the trouble?"

"I've lost my way."

"That's not all you've lost."

"I need this? It ain't bad enough I'm lost, you gotta make jokes? Look, all I want is to get home."

Knuckling the cement walk, he rocked his cart to and fro in front of the welcome mat.

"Hey, sorry about the wisecrack," I said. "Why don't you come in?"

He pressed his right palm flat on the mat and raised his stunted body. He held himself that way, his torso parallel to the ground, like a gymnast on a pommel horse might. Thick veins stood out on his knotty forearm. With his left hand, he grasped the edge of the cart and heaved it over the doorsill onto the floor. He waddled across the threshold on his palms and settle back onto the cart. Not only were his legs missing, I saw on closer inspection, he was cut off above the hips.

"The name's Scooter," he said.

"Pleased to meet you," I replied. "Tell me if I'm rude for asking, Scooter, but how'd you get chopped in two?"

"You're rude for asking. This is the only house on the block with no stoop. Did you know that? That's why I came to you for help."

"What luck."

"It ain't exactly like you hit the Lotto, is it?"

That's when I noticed the man's odor. He stank like the men's room at Yankee Stadium after a doubleheader, on a 100-degree day, when they were handing out free beer. I left the door ajar, opened the windows, and turned on the ceiling fan. As I sat in the easy chair against the far wall, I noticed that my new friend was staring at my undershorts.

"You ain't wearing pants," he said.

"Neither are you," I replied.

"You're a wiseass."

"That's true. So what's your story?"

"Like I said, all I want is to get home. I was

223

working the rush hour crowd on the 7 train last night, panhandling, you understand? That's where I live, the subways. There's these two drunks in suits on the train, see? Working guys, but a drunk's a drunk. Anyhow, when I come rolling up with my cup out, they start laughing. Then I guess they feel bad, see? So they start feeding me beers, had a coupla six packs with them. Hey, I take what I can get."

I was enjoying Scooter's company. It's not every day a fellow like that arrives at your door. The wild expressions he made with his shrunken, pop-eyed face were quite entertaining. For the first time in days, I felt relaxed and forgot about my troubles with Sharon.

"I shoulda known better than to drink them beers," my new friend continued. "Can't handle the stuff. Knocks me right on my ass. So what happens? I pass out. When I come to, I'm in a kitchen. There's music playing. I roll my ass into the other room and find a party goin on. I tap this girl's leg, see? She looks at me like I got three heads. I says, 'where the hell am I?' 'Mark's place,' she says. 'Mark's place in Rockland Park.'"

I sat back and shook my head. Mark is Sharon's ex-boyfriend. He rents a house up the block. Despite the fact that Mark was both physically and verbally abusive to her during their relationship, I had reason to suspect that Sharon had been seeing him again.

"So Mark and his friend abducted you?"

"Yeah, some big fun, huh? Bring a freak to the party, like I'm a circus act. Hey, I wouldn't even complain if they paid me something. Circus acts get paid!"

"Did Mark have a girl with him at the party?" I asked. "A blond with wire-framed glasses and a mole on her right cheek? She'd have been wearing jeans and a white blouse."

"Yeah, she sounds like the one I begged for a ride home. She just gawked at me."

"That bitch," I muttered. My suspicions were confirmed.

"Not one of those bastards would drive me to

the train station, not one!" Scooter shouted. The expression on his face had hardened into a scowl. He shook his finger in the air. "They locked me in the kitchen! I woke this morning beside the trash at the curb!" He pressed his palms flat on the floor behind him, arched his back and began to wail. It was unnerving.

"Get ahold of yourself!" I shouted. I stood and marched forward intent on getting the freak out of my house. In preparation for giving him a great shove, I inhaled deeply. His odor filled my lungs. I stumbled back, gagging, and staggered down the hall to the bathroom where I fell to my knees and puked.

For several minutes I knelt there, my forehead resting on the cool porcelain rim of the toilet, listening to his wailing. When it finally subsided, I returned to the living room. He was sobbing quietly. I couldn't simply shove the poor creature out the door, but why had it fallen upon me to help him? I thought I saw a way out of the predicament that would be satisfying to me in more ways than one.

"Why don't I call the police for you?" I asked. "Mark has violated your rights. Press charges." This got my friend awfully excited. His voice rose to a high, pleading squeal.

"No, please, no!" he begged. "They'll send me to the shelter! They'll get the doctors and head-shrinks pokin' at me. I don't want no trouble. Just get me home."

As much as I relished the idea of seeing Mark behind bars, I didn't want to get Scooter in trouble. Now that he'd stopped bawling, I was beginning to like him again. I decided I'd load him into the back of my minivan and drive him into the city.

"Tell you what, pal," I said. "I'll give you a ride home, but we have to wait until after ten. I'm expecting a call."

He was beaming. The smile on his grotesque face was the most earnest expression of gratitude I have ever seen. I looked away, oddly embarrassed.

"The call you're waiting for?" he asked.

227

"Yeah?"

"It's the blond, ain't it?"

"Yup. We argued early last night and she broke up with me. I told her to sleep on it and call me before work if she has a change of heart. Seeing as how she went straight to Mark's after leaving last night, I suppose I'm wasting my time."

Scooter winked his popeye. "Don't you worry," he said. "Good lookin' fella like you, with both his legs; you'll find another girl in no time. I had me a girl once, years ago you understand. She was a beauty but vicious. Mean as they come. Christ, what she done to me. Makes me tremble just to think of her."

It was impossible to imagine a woman being attracted to my guest, but who knows what sort of a man he might have been before the loss of his lower half and a life of begging had taken their toll on him. I told him I wasn't interested in another girl, that I didn't want to lose Sharon. He scratched the gray stubble on his chin.

"Maybe she'd change her mind if you got her a

228

nice gift and surprised her," he said. The notion of this guy giving me romantic advice struck me as so absurd, I couldn't let it pass.

"What the hell do you know about women, anyway?" I asked.

"Hey, I've looked up more skirts than any man alive!"

That got me. I laughed till I was dizzy at that one, to Scooter's delight. He was grinning, revealing his three jagged teeth. He rocked his cart in short gleeful bursts.

The phone rang. I leapt from the chair, darted into the kitchen, and snatched up the receiver.

"Sharon?"

An enthusiastic recorded voice answered: "How would you like to win a free gift from WKZT, the number one station in all the nation?" Disco music thumped in the background.

I slammed down the receiver and looked at the clock on the stove. Ten-fifteen. I took my key ring down from its hook beside the phone, slipped off the key to Sharon's place, and threw it into the trash can. Then I got a twelve pack of beer out of the refrigerator.

"Have a drink with me, Scooter," I said as I strode into the living room. I held my breath, crossed the room, and handed him a can.

"I shouldn't," he said. He gulped the entire can without stopping. I sat back in my chair and exhaled. Scooter wiped his lips with the back of his hand. I removed another can from the carton and rolled it across the floor to him. He drained it as rapidly as he had the first one. I opened one for myself and rolled him a third.

"Here's to us, pal," I said raising my can. "Let's drown our sorrows."

"What could you possibly know about sorrow?" Scooter asked. A change had come over him. His voice sounded as if it was composed of gravel, ice, and broken glass. The earnest smile of gratitude was gone. His droop-lidded eye was squinched completely closed. His wiry arms were tense. His fists were clenched and pressed to the floor.

"You don't know nothin about sorrow," he said in that menacing voice.

"Hey, my girlfriend dumped me. I think that qualifies me as someone who knows a thing or two about sorrow," I said.

"So she dumped you," he shouted. "Big deal! It ain't like she pushed you in front of a train, is it? No, she didn't push you in front of no goddamn train, did she?" He pointed his finger at me and stared down the length of his arm, with that hideous popeye, as if he was sighting down the barrel of a rifle. "You've got your legs, damn you. You've got your balls! You want to know sorrow? I'll teach you what it means to suffer!"

He jerked a stiletto from one of the pockets of his pullover, pressed the button on the handle, releasing the blade, and held it up for me to get a good look at.

He stuck out his tongue and licked his left hand, then the right. With the heels of his palms, he struck the floor and rocketed toward me, raising the stiletto to the height of my crotch. I jumped and stood on the chair's arms with my back pressed against the wall. The blade pierced the seat cushion, a dead-on shot if I hadn't moved.

Scooter slashed up missing my groin but slicing the flesh of my right thigh. I leapt over him and somersaulted across the floor coming to an abrupt stop against the far wall. I jumped up and turned to run out the door, but my attacker had already slammed it shut and was coming for me. I spun and threw a powerful sidekick which hit him right on the nose. He toppled backward off his cart. I shoved the cart with my heel sending it careening down the long hallway into the kitchen.

I expected to find Scooter sprawled on the floor completely disabled, but when I turned he was running at me on his hands like some monstrous crab. The stiletto, drenched in blood from his shattered nose, was clenched in his mouth. He clamped his wiry arms around my left leg. I could not shake him loose. The punches I threw to his head had no effect. He grasped the stiletto in his right hand and thrust at my groin. I seized his wrist with both hands stopping the progress of the blade just as its tip pierced my undershorts. Holding his fist with one hand and forearm with the other, I pounded his wrist repeatedly against my knee until the stiletto fell to the floor. I kicked it down the hall. That's when I felt his three hideous teeth dig into my thigh.

A bizarre wrestling match ensued which I eventually won. Scooter put up an incredible fight considering his disadvantage. The copious amounts of foul air I was forced to inhale while struggling with him, and the thought of those teeth breaking my skin, turned my stomach. I puked again, this time directly onto my assailant's bloody face, as I held him pinned to the floor. The insanity of my predicament seemed to require an equally insane response. A sort of madness came over me. I reached over and removed a can of beer from the carton.

"So, you tell me you can't hold your drink, hey Scooter? Three cans made you mean, but you say that the stuff knocks you right out. No one would accuse you of having a wooden leg, hey? How many cans does it take my friend?"

"You no good son of a bitch."

"Not going to tell me? Well, I guess I'll simply have to find out for myself. You know, my friend, I'm beginning to think your advice was sound. What my dear Sharon needs is a gift."

Scooter clenched his jaw, but his teeth prevented the gums from making a tight seal. One by one, I poured the cans of beer down his throat until he passed out. I sealed his mouth and taped his arms to his sides with duct tape.

After I bandaged the cuts on my legs and got dressed, I fished Sharon's key out of the trash. I found gift wrap, Scotch tape, and a thank you card in the hall closet. Let me tell you, old Scooter was a sight to see once I got him wrapped up in gold foil and pasted the red bow on top of his head.

I wrote, "Sharon, thanks for a great night," on the card and signed it, "Love, Mark."

Luckily none of Sharon's neighbors were around when I got to her place. I carried Scooter up the stoop and into the house. I left him in the kitchen. As I was about to walk out the door, I turned back for one more look at Sharon's special gift. A large puddle was spreading across the floor. Apparently, Scooter was pissing out all of that beer, although by what means I can't begin to imagine.

Steve Potter is the author of three collections of poetry -- *Social Distance Sing, Mendacity Quirk Slipstream Snafu,* and *Haunted City.* He has been writing nights after work and on the weekends nearly every day for almost forty years.

His writing has appeared in dozens of extant and defunct lit mags including *Blue Collar Review, Chrysanthemum, Drunken Boat, FreeFall, Long Island Quarterly, Midnight Mind, Pacific Rim Review of Books, Pindeldyboz, Thieves Jargon, 3rd Bed, The Raven Chronicles,* and *Stringtown.*

Potter received his MA from Queens College, CUNY. He attended classes at night and worked days driving a plumbing supply delivery van around New York City and Long Island. His stories reflect that dichotomy, inspired as much by the workaday life he's led as they are by the books he's read.

He writes about literature at bookfreak.us and may be reached at stevepotterwrites@gmail.com.